ABOUT DEADSET PRESS

Deadset Press is an independent publisher of incredible speculative fiction. We provide publishing pathways for emerging writers from Australia and New Zealand, and aspire to shine the light on unique and diverse voices.

You can learn more at:

www.deadsetpress.com

ALSO BY DEADSET PRESS

The Zodiac Series

Charity Anthologies

REVOLUTIONS

Australian Speculative Fiction

Edited by Austin P. Sheehan, Grace Chan
& Leanbh Pearson

First published by Deadset Press in 2021.

Cover design Copyright © Pamela Jeffs.

Edited by Austin P. Sheehan, Grace Chan and Leanbh Pearson.

ISBN: 978-0-6450228-3-4

Acknowledgements:

In the spirit of reconciliation, Deadset Press acknowledges the Traditional Custodians of country throughout Australia and their connections to land, sea and community. We pay our respect to their Elders past and present and extend that respect to all Aboriginal and Torres Strait Islander peoples today.

We would like to thank the members of the Australian Speculative Fiction community who submitted many incredible stories, as well as our cover designer Pamela Jeffs, the selection committee, and the fantastic editors Grace Chan and Leanbh Pearson.

— Austin P. Sheehan, on behalf of Deadset Press.

Contents:

The Indelible Imprint of Humans

#

What little is left of my face slips past the socket plugging me into the terminal, fifth from the start of a long row, at the loosely guarded end of the city. Dozens of inhuman eyes watch as pieces of my face slop onto the bench where I have slumped, barely keeping myself upright.

Blood has long stopped servicing the brittle tissues that remain on my frame. Although it's pointless, I can't help but think back to the days when I had bright blue eyes, a smile that dimpled only to the left, a hint of freckles across my nose, and a healthy head of dark hair. My limbs were limber from years of ballet. My mind was once innocent and full of aspirations. None of that remains. Now, gristle that clings to bone, or the tarnished metal which has replaced half my skull. Rods stiffen my arms and legs, and a myriad of bolts connect them. My thoughts are muddied from failure, crushed dreams and heartache.

Robot eyes watch me. They pause in their arbitrary schedules. It's hard for them to pause, I know. They are bound by routine. My intrusion into their world is a spectacle they can't resist.

Humans no longer exist, and to these robots, humans never did. They deleted all the entries, they disposed of all the evidence: flesh and blood, artefacts and treasures. Most of it was catapulted into space, into regions where the debris was already thick and no-one would bother to look for old lifeform rubbish. The proof that humans ever existed is in my existence, as a cyborg, and even I have long been considered myth to them.

The robots stare but don't say anything, or at least nothing that I can hear. The data transmitting between them—their own insubstantial language floating through particles in the air—must be increasing, as they search for the protocols on sighting a cyborg. The only sounds are the crackle of the electricity that keeps them running and the calm rustle of a breeze. The last time anyone spoke to me was decades ago.

* * *

"You can have my eyes," Gill said, as the last of his rotting skin slid from his fingertips. "There's still a good forty years in them."

I didn't want Gill's eyes. My own had a similar time left on them and brown eyes had never suited me. What I wanted was

Gill, alive. My fingers fumbled with the cord as I plugged him into the box beside me, flicked the switches in order and waited while it sucked life from the power grid. It was a cobbled-together piece of junk, but I'd managed to store the essence of four other cyborgs in the box before the robots claimed their bodies for disposal. I hadn't managed to get the box to talk to me, to talk as if my friends were alive, but it showed me memories and moments that they'd stored in long-term data and hadn't the wherewithal to recall.

"Not long now, Gill."

"Bec?" Metal ridges on his brow formed a frown that only another cyborg could spot. Gill frowned when we talked about a single thing and this was not the time to be talking about it. "Don't do it."

I sighed. I'd grown used to the choking sound my sighs made, but that day it rattled me. The rods in my throat tensed. My eyes began to tear. "Please, Gill. This is it. I won't get another opportunity."

"You watch them all day. They're just silly memories. I don't have any memories that you haven't already seen in Roh's, or Kat's, or Bray's, or Nih's. There's nothing else to remember." He choked on the word 'remember'; it was a phlegmy-sounding choke.

Gil's internal tissues were beginning to clog the pipework. Soon the mechanisms would stop moving. Once they stopped,

3

the cerebral system would get the kill signal and I'd no longer have a download window.

"We're over, Bec. There's no spare tissue left. All of us gone."

"I'm not gone."

The box lit up; a green LED flashed in the corner. It was ready. My finger hovered over the button.

Gill sighed. "It will be a torturous march to the grave if you spend it thinking about what . . . once . . . was . . ."

I pressed the button. I would keep Gill forever.

* * *

I played their memories daily, all five sets of them but I favoured Gill's. I re-watched the fall of humans at the hands of their own creations. The dreaded Singularity which humanity feared arrived. I watched as my full-human brethren were poisoned as if they were no better than the cockroaches they had once reviled.

As cyborgs, we were luckier. The robots considered us dirty distant cousins. They tolerated our presence longer. In the beginning, they attempted to convert some of us to whole robots, but the robots found it degrading when those that were converted showed signs of delinquency that didn't suit their regimented sensitivities. They manufactured flesh and bone for us until a mere three centuries ago when they stopped. We were no longer wanted. They watched us slowly die.

There were hundreds of thousands of cyborgs. Many of us died willingly; they had given up; their souls were tormented by visions of better pasts. I was one of many others who fought to stay living. We raided old factories that had been abandoned, yet still maintained their electrical current. Tissue stores and bone depositories were intact, and—though we lacked the knowledge and finesse of our robot doctors—we grafted ourselves as best we could. We were the incarnation of old Frankenstein's monster. There were scars from rough stitches, skin tones that never matched, and awkward finger lengths that made grasping a task of deep concentration and skill. There were plenty of junkyards for our cybernetic structures, though the bits and bobs strewn there were often glitchy. We survived as best we could.

We remained hidden for decades, although, in hindsight, it was pointless. The robot doctors had laced us with cranium tracking devices, ticking time bombs that fused with our cerebral network. They would always find us if they wanted to. The few of us that attempted to sever the link had extinguished themselves, and—within moments—retrieval robots came, scraped their metal frames of flesh, and dismantled them before our eyes. The squeal of scalpels on steel and the sigh of artificial lungs deflating left scarred thoughts haunting my dreams. They took our friends from us in pieces. We knew they'd use their parts, devouring them. Robots are avid recyclers and abhorrent connoisseurs.

I am the last vestige of humanity, and yet the poorest example of it. I look around at the robots that outsmarted us and wonder at how changed the world has become. In a way, it's colder; there's a sense of heartlessness to the endless back-and-forth of the robot civilisation. They don't think; they process. They don't create or design, they build from calculated data. They don't feel.

Yet, outside their pristine grey cities, the world thrives. Animals that had been run down to the brink of extinction now run in packs, wild and free, without a care for how close they'd come to their destruction. The trees are strong and healthy; the seasons are mild and tolerable. Earth appears to be enjoying this new wave of civilisation a lot more than I am. If the robots had welcomed me into their society, would I have accepted?

It's a moot thought; they never offered.

From here, I know they will dispose of me, just as they have my friends. They will scrape the last fragments of tissue from my frame, dismantle my rods and struts and circuitry, and repurpose me.

At the terminal, I can barely keep my head up. The thoughts that are pouring out are cloudy and distant. It's as though my thoughts never existed at all, as though I never existed, as though it were all a fevered dream.

My eyes lose focus. I can no longer see into the real world. My only company is this stream of thought that I am trying to filter into the robots' integral systems, trying one last time to infect them with a human irrationality, and all I see is Gill. It's my favourite memory of us, one that I watched from the box repeatedly. My fingers curl around Gill's broken hand. His tired, brown eyes search mine. He cradles me as his lipless mouth forms the word 'forever'.

About the Author:

Tamantha Smith is an emerging Australian writer of speculative fiction, currently living in Jarowair country, Queensland. She reviews for Aurealis magazine while studying for her Bachelor of Arts (Honours) in Creative and Critical Writing with USQ, working full time in the Royal Australian Navy, and supporting her crazy little family of four.

Tamantha is a passionate introvert that spends half her life inside her own head imagining the future in all its possible woe and glory.

Claws

Sarah Jane Justice

#

Powering face first into the desert, Toby had never experienced such stifling heat. The aging Corolla had been known to struggle at the best of times, enough that keeping the AC turned up had him sweating in anxiety, as well as sunburn. His skin baked under UV rays that blasted through the windshield, and he checked every few minutes to make sure the frail temperature controls were working at all.

He had planned to be settled into his accommodation well before sunset and blamed his miscalculations on the Corolla. Seeing the remaining distance slowly ticking down, Toby's nerves started to get the better of him. When his friends had learned that a rural placement was a compulsory part of his degree, they'd spent weeks winding him up with stories. He'd perfected his poker face through descriptions of the outback's most venomous wildlife, but it was the idea of fitting in with the locals that scared him more than anything. Toby knew that he was the perfect archetype of a city boy, and he could already picture the laughing stares of blokes who had met his type.

In the slow process of fading light, Toby saw the endless stretch of road as a hypnotic vision that made him dizzy. His shirt was damp with sweat, and as the heat slipped into the cold of a desert night, he started to shiver. He could have been gripped with fever and never known it, and when distant lights started flickering ahead, he wondered for a moment if he was just hallucinating.

He slowed down to rub his eyes, struggling to stretch his thoughts back into working order. When the car veered with the movement, he took a moment to pull over and check the map. Relief coursed through him when he confirmed that the lights ahead were real, and his destination was in sight.

He let out a whistle, rolling the tension out of his shoulders until his relief was ripped away in a sudden flash of movement. The car shook with the impact of a beak that smacked against the window. Toby grabbed for the wheel with shaking hands and cursed under his breath. Struggling to keep himself from hyperventilating, he saw the emu staring through his windshield.

The bird stretched to its full height, raising a wiry leg to show off its claws. After lingering just long enough for the glowing eyes to embed themselves into Toby's subconscious, the emu took off, running out into the darkness beyond the road.

* * *

Toby spent the last hour of the drive pleading with the Corolla to keep moving. The car's already straining engine clunked and groaned along the highway until finally, he dragged it into a park on the main street.

"Not sounding too healthy, is she?"

Toby nodded a greeting at the man standing under the awning of the pub, waving him into a park. Toby shut off the engine and stepped out of the car.

The man extended a hand for him to shake. "You must be Toby. We spoke on the phone. I'm Matt," he offered, before stepping closer to the car. "Mmm. Meet a 'roo out there, did you?"

Toby brushed his hand over a deep scratch in the paint that filled his mind with images of claws. "Emu, actually," he muttered, turning away before he could dwell too much on the damage. "Thanks for the room. Anything you need from me before I start lugging my bags up?"

"Bags. Plural, huh," Matt huffed. "Moving in, are you?"

"Didn't want to forget anything, I guess." Toby shrugged.

Matt shook his head with a light-hearted chuckle and reached over to help pull Toby's bags out of the car. As Toby shut the doors behind him, Matt whistled at the fresh scratches in the paint. "So, when you say emu, what do you mean?" he asked. "I swear, you city folk. I can't keep up with the slang."

"Nah, it's not slang," Toby cleared his throat, "It was an emu. A proper one. Jumped right at the car, in the middle of the road. Not far out from here."

Matt shook his head as he led the way towards the pub's side door. "Don't think so. Emus don't attack like that. They're mean buggers if you corner them, but they don't tend to come at you out of nowhere."

"Well this one did." Toby shrugged. "Must have been having a rough day. Lost a bet with the other emus, maybe."

Toby knew how well a light-hearted joke could help in making a good first impression. He was relieved to hear laughter in response.

Shaking his head again, Matt left him with a stern pat on the back, before directing him towards a set of stairs. "Your room's up there" He pointed. "Second on the left. Bathroom and all that have signs on the door. Shouldn't be hard to figure out."

Toby nodded, shaking Matt's hand again before hauling his bags up the narrow staircase.

* * *

Before setting out on the drive, Toby had put a decent amount of time and effort into preparing for the teaching placement that had sent him to such a remote location. With another day left before he started at work, he set to explore the town on foot, an activity that ended up taking no more than twenty minutes. When mid-afternoon faded into evening, Toby stopped counting the number of times he'd walked back and forth along the same stretch of road. Beyond the school, the butcher, and the limited supplies of the general store, the smell of stale, spilled beer that hung over every small-town pub became ever more appealing.

"Toby," Matt waved through the open doors. "Boys, this is our city kid. Doing his uni placement at the school."

The group of men sitting at the bar all looked like they'd sat in the same chairs every day for the last twenty years. As they turned to give Toby a nod and a wave, he saw them as fixtures in this pub, part of the furniture here.

"Thought they were sending a mature age student this time," one of the barflies chuckled.

"Yeah. That'd be me," Toby said, pulling over a stool from a nearby table. "According to them, mature age is anything older than about eighteen. Twenty-four years old, and they're calling me mature age."

"Christ on a cracker," Matt laughed. "If you're mature aged, what does that make me?"

"Not bloody mature, that's for sure," another regular boomed over the foam on his beer. The room broke into raucous laughter.

Looking over his shoulder, Toby was surprised at how fast the dark of night had set in behind him.

Toby peered out of the window at the overwhelming darkness. His friends had told him how much brighter the stars would be without city lights to dull them, but looking outside, Toby would have preferred a few more streetlights. It was much too dark for his tastes, and he had to squint to discern one shape from the next. When his eyes started to hurt from the effort, he suddenly noticed a pair of lights twinkling not far ahead of him. He sat up straight, focusing just enough to make out a stiff, sharp beak, and glaring eyes before they darted off into the distance. Another emu.

"You good, Toby?"

Toby turned to see Matt offering him another beer. "Yeah, good," he shrugged. "Just saw another emu down the street. Didn't look happy, I tell you what. That one from the other night must still owe him money." Toby forced a laugh, immediately hit by a wave of awkward embarrassment when it sounded fake.

"Emus again." Matt shook his head. "I feel like you're setting me up for a prank here, Toby."

"Nah, really," Toby said, straightening up. "It was out there, next to the butcher."

"Yeah, whatever you reckon," Matt laughed, "They are weird looking birds, I will say that. Not real friendly, either."

"They're terrifying," one of the barflies spoke up, "You can say it, we won't think any less of you. They're angry, creepy, bastards of birds."

"Pfft," another man scoffed. "Chickens on stilts. I could take down an emu if I needed to."

With the beer-soaked noise of the crowd rising in volume, it became easier for Toby to shrug off the second emu sighting in as many days. Although the glare of yellow eyes remained in his head, he tried to put it aside. Pushing away from the window, he pulled out his wallet and waved his empty glass in the direction of the bar.

* * *

Toby had made sure to set multiple alarms to help him get out of bed the next morning. He'd turned up late to a few too many 9am classes, and was still trying to find a sound that could drag him out of sleep every time. The piercing scream that woke him up that morning worked better than any alarm he'd ever heard.

Sitting bolt upright, Toby looked around the room in fear and confusion. As the scream broke into gut-wrenching sobs, he jumped across the room and opened the window. A crowd was forming in the street, pulsing with sounds of terror that grabbed at his ears. The noise shattered his last remnants of sleep, echoing as he dressed and ran down the stairs.

* * *

Even in the early hours of morning, the sun was harsh, mixing with the dust in the air to create a thick haze. Rubbing his eyes, Toby pushed his way through the throng of people.

"Stay back," Matt called out from the front of the crowd, "Everyone, pull back. We're sorting it out, you don't want to see it."

Toby rushed forward to where Matt was attempting to herd people away. Behind Matt, a few men and women were huddled around a tarp. On the road, a dark red splatter mingled with the dirt. Toby's stomach turned. "What's going on?" he waved at Matt to get his attention. "What happened?"

When Matt turned to Toby, there was a deep fear shadowing his face, grey creases like arrows aimed toward his eyes, emphasising the burden of what he had seen.

After a quick glance over his shoulder, Matt gestured for one of the other men to take over crowd control, before leading Toby towards the tarp. "You ready?" Matt asked, looking back at him.

Toby nodded, bracing himself for the worst. While he watched the tarp lift, he could convince himself that he was tough enough to handle whatever was under it. In an instant, that reassurance was gone. His eyes landed on the puddle of drying blood before he saw the body. The dead man's face was torn through with deep scratches, and his torso shredded in sharp, distinct cuts. Locked in rigor mortis, his fist was still clenched around a clump of grey feathers.

Matt whispered to the other men huddled around the body. "Those claw marks look like an emu."

"They're foragers," a wavering voice argued. "They don't hunt. They certainly don't hunt humans."

"They never used to," Matt grumbled. "But that's an emu claw, right there. Feathers, too. Unless someone's tried to frame a bloody bird, this was an emu. Something's changed."

Matt stood up and scanned the scene, his eyes landing on Toby. "Hey Toby," he hissed. "You said you saw an emu from the pub last night, right?"

"Yeah," Toby said, pulling himself up. "Standing next to the butcher. Looked like he was staring right at us. Thought I was imagining it."

Matt grunted, wringing his hands as he turned back to look at the tarp behind them. "Something's going on," he muttered. "Something's happened. The—"

A deep, rolling grunt cut him off mid-sentence. The men looked up to see a pair of glowing, yellow eyes staring at them over a beak that clicked with a terrifying sense of purpose. The emu flapped a wing in a sharp, deliberate motion, causing everyone to jump in unison.

Toby froze in a sickening jolt when the emu's eyes landed on him. Its stare was hypnotic, and it dug into him even after the bird twisted its neck towards the rest of the crowd. As it turned, Toby could see a bloody patch on its neck that was bare of feathers, and he remembered the clenched fist of the body under the tarp.

16

CLAWS

His legs trembled as he tried to run, but he was trapped in place. He watched in a trance-like state as the emu raised a claw and sliced through the air. In a swift, sudden movement, the bird charged forward.

Toby heard the screams before he could summon the ability to run. He spun around, his eyes stinging from the dust being churned up into the air. Coughing and spluttering, he saw the pub and started to sprint. The door beckoned to him with the appearance of a barricade, but his bare shreds of hope burst into the flurry of feathers that blocked his path.

He screamed, and the emu stared into him without flinching. It snapped its beak in his face, craning its long neck to display the bloody patch of missing feathers.

Toby stumbled backwards as the emu attacked, his eyes caught in the emu's stare. "Come on," he pleaded with his own shaking limbs. "Just move, come on!"

Blind to his path, Toby collided with another man flailing behind him, and they both fell to the ground. His eyes broke away from the emu, and he swivelled around before climbing back to his feet. For the first time, he saw the rest of the flock.

In every direction, emus were closing on them. They broke the air with vestigial wings that had never been used with such force, waving their claws at the terrified crowd. Toby could sense that he was shifting along the street with the rest of them, but his mind was lost in fear. The bird with the missing neck feathers stood at the front of the flock, staring through the crowd at Toby.

"They're herding us." Matt's voice broke through the air.

"So they're getting us all together." Toby's voice wavered, escaping from his mouth at a much higher volume than he had anticipated. "An Emu buffet with enough meat for all of them."

Matt shook his head. "They don't eat meat."

"Last night you said they don't go out of their way to attack, either," Toby retorted.

A deep grumble echoed through the air as an emu lurched forward, snapping at the space to their right.

Toby stumbled backwards, running with the rest of the crowd, their combined plight making them move in the shape of a single animal. Pushing each other, rushing through rising dust, the townsfolk swarmed towards a sudden gap that had appeared in the circle of emus. Toby recognised the possibility of escape, but couldn't find the strength to take the risk.

"Bugger it!" Matt yelled, breaking through the crowd to dive forward. Toby watched him jump for the gap between the two wayward birds, his breath catching in his throat. He was bracing himself for a blood bath when the birds stepped aside to allow Matt to pass. Strutting in unison, the circle of emus shifted their formation.

Toby's relief was tarnished by an overwhelming sense of dread, but all he could do was move with the other men and women. The emus growled behind them, commanding their direction with the shape of their flock alone.

"The bus." A voice cracked through the air like a whip. "The bus, right there!"

Toby ran along with the rest of the pack, barely able to focus on the rusty tour bus parked at the end of the street. Its roof was flaking off into pieces from years of sitting in one place, decaying under the force of outback sun. Moving as one, the townsfolk clambered on board in a mess of shoving, aching limbs.

"Does this thing lock?" Toby yelled as the door slammed shut behind them.

"What, this piece of junk?" Matt was on his knees, fishing under seats with a fierce determination. "Never needed a lock until just now."

Doused in sweat, men and women pushed their way into the seats, all of them staring out through rusted windows. Toby's eyes blurred with exhaustion, but he gripped the back of a leather seat and stared with the rest of them.

A shiver ripped through his skin as he looked across a sea of glowing, yellow eyes. The emus had them surrounded, their every move calculated like a measured step in a war-like strategy. At the back of the flock, a line of emus returned to the pub, covering further space along the street.

"They're claiming it," Toby muttered, watching every move, "They weren't aiming to kill us at all. They're taking over the town."

"They can have it," Matt grunted, grabbing a rusted ring of keys that had been hidden in a ripped cushion lining. Keys in hand, he lurched towards the driver's seat, forcing the clunky engine into life. Unable to take his eyes away from the scene unfolding around them, Toby watched the emus back away from the bus, blocking the road that led into the town centre.

Matt revved the engine and sent the bus screeching away from town. One by one, the townsfolk looked away from the windows and sat down. They rubbed their eyes and clutched their chests, some still whimpering under their breath.

"They beat us. They formed a plan, and they beat us. Flightless birds." Toby shook his head, "Guess that's one way for them to rise up." He chuckled to himself, considering the possibility that the rich blend of relief and exhaustion had sent him delirious. He knew that the joke would be ignored, but he was too far past the point of caring.

As the bus drove further away, a rising flurry of feathers rose above the town which almost resembled a flag.

Dedicated to the brave soldiers who fought in the Great Australian Emu War of 1932

About the Author:

Sarah Jane Justice is an author, poet, and performer working on Kaurna land. Her poetry has been featured in releases from The Blue Nib, Capsule Stories, and Pure Slush, and her short fiction has been published by Hawk and Cleaver, Eerie River Publishing, and Black Hare Press.

In addition to the written word, Sarah is also an award-winning spoken word artist, whose credits include performing at the Sydney Opera House as a national finalist in the 2018 Australian Poetry Slam.

The Ballad of Dallas Brand

Stephen Herczeg

\#

"Out here in the rim worlds, our legends are many, our heroes are few," said Uncle Alstar to the younglings at his feet.

The gathered group enjoyed the evening story telling. They crowded around the small fire; each one focused on every word.

"There is a new tale that lives on in the minds of many. The story of Dallas Brand. The revolutionary. The outlaw. The criminal."

Several of the children let out a small gasp. They had only ever heard the name spoken but in whispers from their parents. It was a name that struck fear in the hearts of men, and now Alstar was going to tell them his story.

"There are some that say Brand came from old Earth. There are others that say he was a demon made flesh. And there are others that say he was from an undiscovered alien species. No-one wants to know the truth, even Brand keeps it hidden. Brand is a man, but a man like no other. Every ounce of his essence radiates power. He stands head and shoulders above all others. His fury is like the power of a sun made flesh."

Not a peep came from the assembled children, their tiny, upturned faces fixed on Alstar, their mouths open, unspeaking.

"If you fell to the wrong side of Dallas Brand, then your life would be short and full of pain."

Several adults nearby looked across and smiled. Alstar had a knack of keeping the children quiet and entertained for hours.

No-one knew where Alstar came from. He appeared in their camp several years ago. Bedraggled, dehydrated, starving, and half-dead. They took him in, and he repaid them with knowledge of the old ways. He fixed the ancient machines, which helped improve the cropping yield. The whole community reaped the benefits of his presence and wisdom. To them he was a hero. To the children he had become a legend.

"Many people thought they knew what drove Brand. They say he wanted to cause an upheaval in the galactic order. A rebellion. He inspired mutinies amongst the downtrodden. Drove them to riots, overthrowing those in power. But none knew him. He didn't want any of that. What lay in his heart was nothing short of pure evil. He enjoyed the pain, the death, the destruction and the terror that he brought."

Several of the adults became concerned. This was a much darker story than others, and some of the little faces wore

23

expressions of growing horror. As Dariud, the leader, stepped towards the ring of light to put a stop to the story, a shape strode from the darkness and blocked his way.

Fire light gleamed off bright metal. Dariud couldn't tell if it was a helmet or part of the figure's skull. As the strange head turned to Dariud, a bright green light passed over his eyes, scanning him, translating Dariud's features and form into information that was fed to the brain within.

Dariud shrank back in terror, as though his very soul had been absorbed by the figure. Together, Dariud and the small crowd of villagers drew back towards their houses.

A small hand shot into the air from one of the children. "Uncle? How do you know so much about Dallas Brand?"

Alstar's mouth opened to answer, but a deeper, hoarse voice cut in.

"Alstar ran with Brand for many years. He was one of his chief lieutenants. Isn't that right, Varmind Alstar?" the tall figure asked, his boots crunching on the gravel as he stepped into the circle of light.

Alstar peered up into a face he hadn't seen in over a decade. He recognised the man; they had once been friends. But from the expression on that grizzled face, that was no longer the case. "Maygist?"

"I've been looking for you, Alstar," said Maygist. He pulled a small plastic card from a pocket in his chest armour and held it out. "The Galactic Council has issued a warrant for you." His other hand rose holding a deadly plasma pistol.

The old man stared at the sparkling tip of the gun pointed at his face. "We were friends once. I would have died for you."

"You made your choice. Anyone who sides with Brand has been condemned by Council decree."

Alstar nodded, he'd known this day would come. "I'm telling the children the ballad of Dallas Brand. Can I at least finish my story?"

"I'll be the one to finish that story."

The shimmering barrel of the pistol flashed once, bringing an end to Varmind Alstar and darkness to Dariud's little community.

* * *

Baddoom spun at the edge of the outer rim, a sparkling jewel in the crown of the Galactic Council. It was the only producer of ionised bavarium, the source of power for every ship in the Council's fleet. Detected a hundred years before, the planet seemed nothing more than a desolate rock. An accidental discovery of the innate ability of its prime mineral, bavarium, to harness the immense power of its electron makeup, set off a new age of space travel.

This new power source fuelled an advanced type of star drive which could fold space, allowing ships to leap light years in mere hours rather than months.

Following in his father's footsteps, Sandar Goskin joined the bavarium plant security team straight out of school. A dull job, but it was stable and paid well. Something his wife was thankful of. His feet hurt from the long shift as he stared at the soaring bavarium ionisation towers. Lightning arced between them as the raw ore raced along the enrichment lines inside.

He shifted the weight of his gun as another bolt of lightning left a blinding trail across his vision. It wasn't Sandar's job to understand the complex scientific process. He was a guard but had heard the techs talk about changing molecular structures and added extra electrons or something. *Tech stuff. Way above my pay scale.*

Movement further down the gantry caught his eye. A shadow was thrown onto the tall processing chamber wall. A figure stepped around the corner, and headed towards Sandar, head scanning from side to side, a gun held at the ready.

Sandar relaxed as he recognised Demorg, who had been sharing this shift with him for the last two weeks. Tensions had heightened since an outpost on nearby Karrack was destroyed by Brand and his band of rebels.

Another violent flash of lightning lit up the area, snatching Sandar's attention. It was a sight that never failed to impress.

Expecting Demorg to be close by, Sandar glanced along the metal gantry. It was empty. A tingle ran up his spine, his senses pulsing on full alert.

A dark figure stepped into the light. Dressed in black from head to foot, it held a tube-like weapon, raised at the ready. The intruder's head turned towards him, eyeing Sandar as if waiting for some signal.

Sandar lifted his rifle, ready to fire. A tiny click sounded behind him, and full of terror, Sandar froze.

"Put it down little man."

Sandar half-turned, staring up at the towering man behind him. The menacing figure of Dallas Brand held a blaster at Sandar's head. With his other hand, he aimed a plasma launcher at the ionisation towers.

"No!" Ejaculated Sandar. "You can't. You'll destroy everything. My family depends on that plant. Just take the bavarium, you don't have to destroy it all."

"I don't want the bavarium. I want to stop the fleet. You gotta better idea, I'd love to hear it," came the smiling reply.

The plasma launcher fired, a jet of fire streaking from the barrel towards the ionisation towers. Within seconds the night sky of Baddoom lit up in a brilliant blinding flare of blue light.

In the afterglow, Sandar caught his first good glimpse of Dallas Brand. His mouth dropped open as he stared at the three-metre-tall hulking giant before him. His shoulders were twice as broad as Sandar's, and his face looked carved from ancient stone, with a bristling black beard hanging down to his chest.

Brand turned his gaze from the show in the heavens down to Sandar with a leering grin. "Now, I don't usually kill folk unless they tries to kill me first." Brand said.

"Me either," coughed Sandar, his squeaky voice betraying his fear.

"So, you've got a choice to make. You can join my cause. Or not."

Sweat prickled on Sandar's forehead, beads running down into his eyes. Blinking them away while staring at the steel gun barrel, one thought came to mind.

This shit is way above my pay scale.

* * *

Tantarus, a jump station halfway between Baddoom and the outer rim, was a shithole of a planet. Cold, with an almost continuous rain of water, diluted calcium hydroxide and sodium peroxide, which stung unprotected skin and eyes.

As humans spread throughout the galaxy, Tantarus had taken on a life for itself, both as a transport hub and a lair for criminals and smugglers. Law enforcement didn't care how Tantarus was run or who occupied it, just as long as the traffic ran free, they left it to itself.

Being a home for criminals, Tantarus became a beacon for bounty hunters like Locke. Word had come across the sat-net that Dallas Brand had arrived on Tantarus, and the attack on

Baddoom's bavarium plant had caused the *Doghouse* to become a hive of activity.

The *Doghouse* was the large station used by the bounty hunters for administration and as an intermittent home base between assignments. The Galactic Council had built it and deployed it in orbit around Altair IV, a planet near the interstellar transport routes connecting the outer rim and inner sanctum.

Rather than send troops or employ a police force to uphold law and order across the rim worlds in its infancy, the Council had instituted a decree and amnesty to petty criminals that if they signed on as bounty hunters their records would be erased.

Blowing on her coffee in the *Doghouse*'s servery, Locke's wrist computer vibrated with the contract update. The Council were not amused; the Chairman had tripled Brand's bounty when he had heard of the latest attack. A smile grew across Locke's face as she read the updated figure. She knew Brand, she had feared Brand ever since she'd fled his increasingly bizarre rants and ravings about bringing down the Galactic Council.

In the beginning, it has been a bit of fun. She was young and impressionable, and robbing a few rich wayfarers across the outer rim worlds sounded like an amusing way to live. And it had been. That's where she'd met Maygist. Within weeks they were bonded, and she gave him the one thing she possessed that she was happy to lose. They'd skipped out on Brand and his men in the middle of night. As outlaws, their only hope of a future was to become bounty hunters. The Council stretched the rules concerning those who were risking their lives as law keepers. The bounty hunters were a substitute police force, operating just inside, and sometimes outside, the law.

Brand had remained in Locke's mind for the past few years. Someone to fear and avoid, until the price was right. Maygist had warned her off tracking him down, but the latest contract had put him in her sights.

On her way to Baddoom, Locke had received the update about Brand's presence on Tantarus. She changed course, and soon touched down on this god forsaken chunk of rock.

As it turned out, Locke was alone. No other hunter had landed on Tantarus at that point in time. Lucky for her.

Unlucky for Brand.

It had taken several days of trawling the local bars and dives—gathering information, through overhearing snippets, to bribery, to threats at knifepoint—to learn about Brand's whereabouts, but now Locke was confident she had him.

Standing beneath the eaves of a dilapidated house, Locke stretched her metal hand into the rain shower. The knuckle joints whirred as she flexed her fingers, washing away the blood. The man lying dead at her feet had once been one of Brand's helpful associates.

Peering through the teeming rain, Locke spied movement in the upper floor of the building. Two figures in front of the windows cast a shadow puppet show across the translucent blinds. The bigger shadow had to be Brand, his hulking form would fill those windows and more.

As the lights were extinguished, Locke tensed. They were on the move. It was time.

A moment later, a sliver of light appeared under the doorway. Locke's hand dropped to her hip, the plasma pistol melding with her metallic hand in a symbiotic dance of death.

The door opened wide, and as the shadow emerged, Locke aimed at the darkness in the doorway. An itch registered in her metal hand, a phantom irritation where flesh had once been. She winced at the prickling feeling; one she hadn't felt in years. One that only happened when she was in danger.

Locke froze. Cold metal pressed against the nape of her neck, chilling the bare skin beneath her hat. "Fuck," she said under her breath.

"Hello Locke, it's bin a while, hasn't it?" A deep voice drawled through the drizzle. "Now, why would a bounty hunter be swanning about in the rain on this mud-heap?"

Locke turned, staring up into the single eye of death pointed at her forehead. The colossal form standing before her filled her mind with fear. Brand was even taller than she

31

remembered. Her eyes climbed up his enormous frame, stopping at his aged face a full metre above her own.

Brand smiled down at Locke, a toothy grin that shone white beneath his thick black beard. "Now Daria, we've known each other for years, but I reckons this ain't no sociable visit, is it?"

Locke couldn't stop herself from shaking her head. There was something in this man's presence that dragged obeyance from you.

"Thought not." Brand paused, drawing a long breath, his voice almost a whisper, forcing Locke to concentrate on his words. "I was very upset when you and Maygist left our happy little band. Now that you've become a bounty hunter, I'm plain disappointed, and I gettin' sick of you scumbags following me everywhere. It's making it very difficult to achieve my aims."

"What aims?"

Brand smiled again; a wide white glow framed by a bushy black border. "I'm gonna bring down the Council, that's what."

"You'll never do it," Locke sighed. "They'll stop you."

Brand shook his head. "They'll try, but by the time they stop sending insects like you after me and bring in the big guns, I'll have brought down most of their might. Now, as I said, we've known each other for years, but I can't be seen as weak, so I've got one thing left to say to you."

"What?" Locke asked, a sense of dread overtaking her.

"You're toast."

Brand squeezed the trigger.

* * *

Stepping back on board the *Doghouse* for the first time in four weeks, Maygist looked forward to cashing in his ticket on Alstar, then downing a large amount of it at the saloon on level six.

His other hope was that Daria Locke had arrived back as well. They had a strange relationship, one that crossed paths from time to time, but when it did, the complaints from neighbouring sleep pods were many. Maygist and Locke were close but being in each other's pockets wasn't something either wanted, so they worked alone and found each other on occasion.

Maygist's first stop was to cash in the ticket. He stepped into the *Doghouse's Pulpit*, so called because it was where the local chief made announcements and read, to the collected bounty hunters, the daily sermon on punishing misdeeds.

The opposite wall was covered in viewscreens showing a continual list of known criminals and the amount on their heads. Another wall was lined with the intelligence points. These computers could be accessed by the bounty hunters to track down suspects, watch news-vids and book transport to the nearby systems.

Maygist passed the plastic card through the slot in the adjacent plasti-glass screen. A scarred and burnt face took one look at the card, picked it up and inserted it into a nearby machine. A small screen showed a three-dimensional image of Varmind Alstar, a five-figure sum and 'DECEASED' flashing beneath.

Damaron, the money keeper, looked up into Maygist's weary face, focusing on the one good eye and avoiding the green cybernetic lens. "Alstar? Weren't you and he friends going way back?"

"Once." Maygist nodded. "He had the same choice as me. He took the wrong one."

Damaron tapped several icons, transferring the bounty to Maygist's account. "You're a hard man Maygist, I'll give you that. Wouldn't want to come on the bad side 'a ya."

Maygist nodded. He'd built a reputation. It didn't make him many friends, but it kept him alive. With the money he made, he could buy friends-if he wanted any. "Has Daria Locke checked in?"

Damaron dropped his head and pointed to the large view-screen at the far end of the room. "Check out the latest intel."

Confused, Maygist peered at the screen. It showed a vid-news report with a large headline *Brand Targets Military Depot on Tantarus*. A presenter appeared to read the report. "The self-proclaimed new Emperor of the Galaxy, Dallas Brand, released a statement to the press saying that yesterday's attack on the ammunition depot, which followed the destruction of the Baddoom bavarium enrichment plant, was the beginning of the poor and disenfranchised rising up to take back what was theirs." The video changed to show the Emperor flanked by members of the Galactic Council. *It must be serious.*

"After the Baddoom travesty, the Council has increased the bounty on Brand's head by threefold. Today, I have increased that by a factor of ten. I pledge that Brand *will* be brought to justice. I am mobilising the Galactic Force to hunt Brand and his followers. I have also passed a decree that any citizen providing proof that Dallas Brand has been executed can request payment, but they must have significant proof."

Turning back to Damaron, Maygist held up his hands. "What's that got to do with Daria?"

Desperate to avoid answering Maygist's question, Damaron busied himself, his back to the bounty hunter.

"Damaron, I don't want to get upset, but I will if you don't answer me." The tone of Maygist's voice had such an underlying threat that Damaron relented and turned around. He pointed towards the intel vid-screens. "Check the sat-net. I warned her, honest I did, but Locke always did things her own way."

A prickle of fear ran up Maygist's back, something so alien to him that his passive expression threatened to buckle. Slowly, he turned to the vid-screens.

He approached the nearest sat-net console and entered Locke's name into the search engine. Several articles from the Galactic news feed appeared, including one from the *Doghouse*'s internal information broadcast system. As Maygist read, the bottom fell out of his world.

"Dead? How could she be dead?" Maygist yelled after the money-keeper.

A single tear appeared in Maygist's good eye and tracked down his scarred cheek.

Why? Why would she go after Brand on her own?

Tears streamed down one side of Maygist's face. He put a forearm against the screen and sobbed the grief out of his system.

Another bounty hunter entered the *Pulpit*, but when he saw Maygist hunched over in grief and fury, he retraced his steps as quietly as he could. Maygist's rage was well known throughout the *Doghouse*, and news of Daria's demise had run through the place like lightning. Nobody wanted to broach the subject with Maygist, nobody that valued their own life, at least.

* * *

It was a weeklong journey from the *Doghouse* to Keppler II, a barren piece of rock, circling twin suns, at the innermost edge of the outer rim. The intelligence Maygist had obtained placed Brand and his group at Keppler.

Despite the intense sun and heat, the planet had proved habitable, with deep veins of dilurium and antrium, two metallic ores used in the manufacture of medical implants, attracting, first the Empire's and now the Council's continued attention.

He'd never been here, but Maygist owed his own survival to Keppler's thriving mining colony. Using dilurium implants, the Military doctors had put him back together, otherwise he would have been just another casualty of the rim wars.

Maygist sat in the galley of his ship, the *Blitzspear*, a contour map of the planet displayed on the table that served as a view-screen.

So far in his campaign, Brand had targeted Council installations vital to continue their push into new territories. If Brand was on Keppler, the ore extraction plants must be his next target.

It's the dilurium.

At the thought of the rare metal, Maygist felt an ache in his articulated hand. The ache throbbed in that phantom limb, lost years before and replaced with a dilurium appendage. Flexing the shiny fingers, he longed to feel again with human digits, but those days were gone forever.

Staring at his metallic hand, Maygist couldn't help thinking that Brand targeting Kepler made more sense if he was after revenge. There were bigger military targets, but both Maygist and Locke relied on dilurium. To Maygist, this was simply pay back against Locke and himself for escaping Brand's group and having the audacity to return for Brand's bounty.

Maygist didn't care about the bounty anymore. He was after vengeance. Brand hadn't needed to kill Locke, Maygist was sure of that, it was all part of what made Brand tick. The power and violence. The sadistic thrill of inflicting pain, of killing. Maygist had seen it in Brand all those years ago. It was part of the reason he'd left. The deaths, the torture, the violence for no apparent purpose. Brand was returning to form.

The more Maygist read about Brand's "enlightened quest" to rid the galaxy of the Council, the more Maygist realised it for the façade it was. Brand was Brand, and always would be. A run-of-the-mill homicidal maniac that relished the chance to injure, kill, and inflict pain. He wasn't a messiah; he was just a killer.

Poring over the map of the northern continent, where the richest deposits were found, Maygist's eyes fell on Dahclune, a frontier town that serviced the biggest dilurium mine on Keppler. The outlying country consisted of interconnected rocky valleys, perfect for hiding a large contingent of freedom fighters.

Running a search across any known associates of Brand and Keppler, a single name displayed. Maygist read the name and smiled, it was an old acquaintance, one he would be very happy to rekindle.

Taylor.

* * *

"I ain't seen Brand, honest, Maygist, I ain't seen him in years."

Maygist grabbed Taylor by the throat and slammed him against the wall of the hovel he'd dragged him from. His optical implant scanned the squirming man's vital signs sending them straight into Maygist's brain. "Your heart's racing and your temperature's rising. I can hear you panting. There's sweat beading on your forehead. Something's scaring you, Taylor, and I doubt it's me."

"Of course, it's you! I've always been scared of you, 'specially now you is a *dog*. I still got a price on my head, why shouldn't I be scared of you?"

"Your ticket says *Dead or Alive*, and the price is only four figures, you're only just worth my trouble. Nah, it's Brand. He's got you foxed like he had all of us. I'm not too man to say he scared the fuck out of me once too, but those days are long gone." Maygist drew his pistol from its holster and brought it up to Taylor's face.

Taylor's eyes went wide with terror. "You don't have to kill me."

"I won't if you tell me where he is."

Taylor's mouth moved as he fought against his fear. Maygist knew the hold Brand had on him; say nothing and risk dying at Maygist's hands or tell the bounty hunter everything and die by

Brand's. The little man's eyes darted to the right, just as a boot crunched on the dry dirt of the road.

Such a heavy footstep could only come from one man.

Maygist spun, dropping Taylor and pointing his weapon towards the new arrival.

Shit.

At least twenty rifles and pistols were aimed at him. Maygist dropped his gun and scanned the crowd, but the towering hulk of Dallas Brand was nowhere to be seen. These were just the Dahclune townsfolk he'd seen over the last couple of days. Folk he'd talked to, trying to tease out details of Brand's whereabouts. He'd lucked into seeing Taylor as the man arrived in town that morning.

Ganthar, Dahclune's de-facto leader stepped forward. He was a pudgy, swarthy man about fifty years old, with ruddy cheeks and a sparse growth of course hair on his round head.

Holding his empty hands out, palms up, Maygist watched Ganthar. He didn't like his odds but started with the official line. "What's going on here? I'm bound by the Council's orders to bring justice to criminals like Taylor here. Such opposition is in direct conflict the Council's orders."

Ganthar's smile showed a lack of teeth. "We don't care about the Council's orders, or asshole dogs like you. Your days are numbered. Pretty soon there's gonna be a change." The assembled townsfolk nodded and murmured their agreement. "Brand says we'll be taking over when it all goes to shit."

Brand. He's got into their heads. Damn.

"Brand won't even make it to Earth. The Council have ordered the military to deal with him. He'll be dead within weeks."

"If that's so, why are you here?"

Maygist's face darkened anger brewing within him. "For me it's personal," he spat. "Let me get on with it. If Brand kills me then I won't be your problem anymore."

Using slow and exaggerated movements, Ganthar drew a long blade from a sheath at his belt. Stepping forward, he waved it from side to side, catching the sunlight and flashing it across Maygist's face, blinding his human eye. Maygist ignored it as the ocular implant scanned Ganthar. Heart rate was normal, blood pressure normal, no undue sweating or breathing, the man was calm, contented, fully induced by Brand's ideology. Far more dangerous than a fanatic.

Stepping backwards, away from the knife, pain burned through his skull as his back hit the little hovel's hot wall.

"We've had problems with people like you ever since the Council landed on this rock," Ganthar said. The crowd behind murmured their agreement. Harsh voices shouted out, calling for the bounty hunter's blood. A shot rang out, smacking into the wall near Maygist's head. His gaze distracted by the impact, quick movement to the side caught him off guard. Ganthar stepped rapidly forward, the blade flashing once more.

Maygist screamed.

* * *

Maygist stumbled into the main street. Dust clouds rose around him, stirred by his shuffling and the desert wind.

This is a shitty place to die.

Hand clamped against the pain in his abdomen, Maygist searched the information filling his mind from his implant and headed for the suggested escape route. The desert. His hope was to lose himself and wait until he recovered enough to seek help or make it back to the *Blitzspear*. No help existed in this town, only the promise of more pain.

Brand wouldn't allow him the luxury of vanishing to fight another day. The townsfolk had already joined his fight. Ganthar's knife had disabled Maygist, making him easy prey. Their absence now meant one thing. The hunter was on his way.

Stumbling in a deep rut, Maygist cursed, his momentum driving him to his knees. A scream leapt from his throat as his insides tore further. His hand dropped from the wound in his stomach, the bulging loops of intestines released into the world, filling his nostrils with their putrid stench.

Blood-slimed loops of flesh uncoiled and spilled across the ground. Agony fired through Maygist's core as his organs fell onto the dusty road. Forced by the pain and nausea, the contents of his stomach emerged into the daylight, bile and half-digested steak splattering down his chest and the pile of dirt-covered intestines.

The agony of his exposed innards, mixed with the force of his convulsions, threw dark patches over his consciousness. Maygist fell forward into the stinking pile, rolling onto his side. Fresh agony ripped through him, and as he gasped air into his lungs, the stink of the vomit and blood threatened to make him wretch again.

Heavy footsteps approached where Maygist lay, and his heart sank. This time there was no mistaking who they belonged to. They were the unmistakable footfalls of the man he had come to kill.

If he could, Maygist would have kicked himself for his stupidity. Vengeance never worked. They always said you should dig two graves. Now he just hoped they gave him the benefit of his own.

Love and loss had made him foolish. Every other hunter rejected the thought of tracking and killing Dallas Brand. The walls of the *Doghouse* were littered with the pictures of those who had chosen to hunt Brand and failed. If it hadn't been for Daria's, Maygist would have left Brand to the military. The thirty million on Brand's head had been tempting, but it was an afterthought. Now he would be the latest in Brand's long line of victims.

43

The hard footsteps stopped near his collapsed form. Maygist shifted, wincing in pain, but focused on the dark form standing above him. Data scrolled his inner eye relating facts he knew by heart. Three metres of pure evil towered above, lit by the light of this world's twin suns.

"Geez, you stink, Maygist." Brand's voice was deep and harsh. "I thought you would have learnt all those years ago. Anyone who crosses me ends up dead in the dirt."

"You didn't have to kill Daria."

A deep, crackling sound split the silence. Brand was chuckling to himself. "Yeah, I guess I didn't have to kill her, but it brought you to me. That saved me a lot of trouble."

"Why? Why did you want me?"

"I need to send a message to all you dog scum. Plus, you pissed me off when you left, Maygist. Nobody leaves my gang." Brand thumped his chest. "I take that sort of disloyalty very personally. Besides, I'm building an army here and I need all the good soldiers I can get. You were one of the best, but you turned on me. And now you're back, trying to take me on."

Brand reached down, dragging Maygist up by his chest armour. Another cascade of organs slipped from his abdomen, splattering Brand's boots with gore. He looked down at the mess and chuckled again. "You done dirtied my boots." A wide grin crossed his face. "I would have said you didn't have the guts to take me on once, but from the look of you, you've proved me wrong."

Maygist sneered between grimaces. "You're insane. Always have been. The Council will kill you before you get within ten lightyears of Earth."

A wide grin broke across Brand's face. "I don't think so. Who do you think's financing my little operation?"

A confused expression crossed Maygist's face. "I don't understand."

"There are people. Some high up people that don't like what's been happening. They need someone like me to change things while they hide in plain sight. It's a shame, I could have used someone like you, but it just wasn't to be."

Maygist tried to reply but stopped when Brand pushed the barrel of his gun against Maygist's cybernetic lens.

As Brand thumbed the hammer back on the ancient gun, Maygist shut his human eye, enjoying a moment of silence.

The *crack* of the gun echoed across the barren, rocky desert.

About the Author:

Stephen Herczeg is an IT Geek, writer, actor, film maker and Taekwondo Black Belt from Canberra, Australia, who has been writing for well over twenty years, with sixteen completed feature length screenplays, and numerous short and micro-fiction stories. Stephen's scripts, TITAN, Dark are the Woods, Control *and* Death Spores *have found success in international screenwriting competitions with a win, two runner-up and two top ten finishes.*

He has had over sixty short stories and seventy micro-fiction drabbles published through Hunter Anthologies; Things In the Well; Blood Song Books; Dragon Soul Press; Oscillate Wildly Press; Black Hare Press; Monnath Books; Battle Goddess Productions; Fantasia Divinity and Deadset Press. A growing number of his Sherlock Holmes and H.G. Wells inspired tales have found favour with Belanger Books and MX Publishing.

His first collection of Sherlock Holmes stories, The Curious Cases of Sherlock Holmes *has just been published, and his first novella,* After the Fall, *will follow in July this year.*

He lives by the creed "Just Finish It" and his Mum is his biggest fan.

Talismans

Leanbh Pearson

#

The standing stones had always terrified me, but now I could not recall why. Two men led me by my bound wrists, yet I followed docile and unconcerned by the procession around me. Above the mountain ridge, the sky arched in a vast black expanse painted with stars, the autumn breeze without chill. Focusing on the path ahead, the incline rose toward the mountain peaks. There, the golden moon illuminated a cluster of standing stones on the plateau between rocky crags.

Staring at the moon, the first awareness of fear roused within me. The flaring torches marked the path to where a bonfire waited in the centre of the stone circle. Fear pricked me again. My heart thudded, wildly, like unsynchronised drums and I wanted to flee, caring nothing for the great hunter, the Horned One. I was not a sacred warrior to this dark god. I tried to turn, my limbs clumsy and slow. A mass of masked dancers pressed me, preventing my escape. Trapped, I clenched my fists, lifting them, preparing to fight. But it was folly, I was scarcely more than a child.

Strong hands caught my shoulders and arms, pinning me. Struggling against my restraints, heart pounding in a staccato rhythm, the anthropomorphic figures surrounded me, pressing closer, faces hidden by masks decorated with antlers, talons, fangs and claws. Panicked, my sight blurred as I was dragged towards the bonfire. There, trembling from exhaustion, I sagged to my knees, head hanging, I let the night air cool my sweaty skin. Desperately, I tried not to hear the invocation to the dark god, nor see the shifting figures silhouetted against the firelight.

A loud drum vibrated through the night. Jolted back to awareness, I searched the dancers in their masks and painted skin, fur capes swaying hypnotically. My Chieftain stepped toward the bonfire, the great curved horn raised to his lips and, as he blew, the summons echoed through the mountains like a battle cry.

A female voice answered, clear and unwavering. The drumbeat quickened, writhing silhouettes of dancers parting to reveal the witch. Not the wizened crone I had been taught to fear since childhood, she was young, her body lithe, movement graceful as she walked between dancers, limbs tattooed with the sigils of her craft. Dressed in a simple skirt made from the same pale buckskin as my own pants, the pelt from a white arctic wolf around her shoulders was stark in the moonlight.

TALISMANS

She raised an ornate bronze bowl to the sky and knelt before me, a clay bowl of smouldering herbs in her hands. Blue smoke curled around me and I stared into her dark eyes, the heady smoke relaxing. Instinctual fears became whispers as I struggled to keep my eyes open. She moved the large bronze bowl in front of me, handing the clay bowl and its intoxicating mixture to a worshipper.

I watched, mesmerised as firelight flickered on the bronze bowl, a constellation engraved in its centre, symbolising the most ancient of the gods, the Horned One with power over life and death, over mortals and lesser gods alike. Dully, I thought how much the sigil looked like antlers cast against a swollen moon. Fear struck me then, cold and certain. And I stared at the witch as though seeing her for the first time, her fingers slick with blood as she placed a long blade down. Without comment, she withdrew, fresh gouts of my blood now filling that bowl, covering the sigil of the dark god.

Realisation struck me like a blow. But I was too late. My blood pulsed from my ruptured throat, the sharp pain overwhelming my other senses. I fought the bonds on my wrists, desperate to lift my hands to my throat, to somehow stem the fatal flow. *Oh gods, someone stop the bleeding. Someone help me.* I mouthed, voiceless and silent. Strength was leaving me with each furious pump of my heart, bringing me closer to death.

The witch walked away, cradling the bronze vessel, its contents sloshing over the rim. Steadying herself, she lifted the bowl in upraised arms, honouring the starry sky and the hunter's moon above. Around her, the dancers parted, horned and antlered beings shifting in the firelight with predatory grace.

The grip of my silent captors weakened. Easing me to the ground, I scrabbled weakly against the mossy earth, blood soaking into the grass with the last of my life. The revellers continued to dance, unheeding of my choked whispers Around me, the shadows drew closer.

The flaring golden light of the bonfire dimmed as the witch called forth an invocation. A final drumbeat echoed through the mountains, resolute, as first light pierced the eastern horizon.

In answer, my own heart stuttered and stopped.

* * *

Every lore I had ever been told assured me that the dead could not linger in daylight. In the final moment of death, when spirit and body separated, I longed to evanesce like morning mist with the first touch of sunlight. But I did not. Instead, I was an incorporeal presence among the standing stones, forced to watch, voiceless and enraged, as the masked worshippers departed. Staring down at my discarded body, the chill autumn air already cooling it.

Ignoring the last of the dancers, the witch continued her whispered prayers before the bonfire, lips repeating invocations to her wretched antlered god. Rage curdled within me, stirring a desire to punish those from my own village who had offered me to the witch's magic. But without body or voice, I could do nothing but observe the witch slowly exhale. She cast furtive glances about the deserted clearing before she walked to my body with a reverence that horrified me. I understood in that moment how her magic had bound my spirit to this world, preventing the evanescence I needed to rescue me from the brutality of my death. Hatred welled within me; an intensity I never knew possible.

The witch lifted the long bronze blade she had used to cut my throat. Whispering a prayer above the blade, she turned to my corpse and her grisly task. I endured the bloody labours of her ritual, refusing to turn aside from the desecration of my own flesh as it was stripped from my bones. Listening throughout the daylight hours to the solemn chanting of her invocations, my anger hardened into a weapon she could never break. She worked without rest, arms bloodied with her efforts, my body reduced to parts, to blood, sinew, muscle, and bone.

Stoking the coals of the bonfire, she encouraged embers to flame and placed the ritualised pieces of my body upon the pyre. Exhausted and dulled with a miserable ache, I watched her purify each item of my body, marking the sigils of her craft with my blood or ash, each rune a burning brand carved into my spirit. When sunset drew close and the last of the light drained from the sky, she lifted a bronze pendant into the air, inspecting her work. It was imbued with the power of her craft. The sigils of her binding magic were within the burnt bone, scorched hair, and preserved muscle that she had fastened to the pendant.

The magic of her bindings was like rope, tying my spirit to this earth through the talisman she now hung around her neck. Staring in horror at those sigils she had carved into my burnt bone, into the talisman itself, were now writ across my incorporeal form.

She turned to stare at me and touched her lips to the grisly talisman she wore, before whispering a command. "Anlan."

In that single summons, she named me by my true name, that which I had been called in life, and had greatest power over me. And I understood with contemptuous outrage, the horror she had made of me. Not only had she had stolen the vitality of my life, the promise of youth, and offered it as sacrifice, she had perverted who I had been, maiming my spirit as surely as she had desecrated my body.

Rage swelled within me, awakening another power with its ignition. Something crafted, untested, and wild burned within me. The powerlessness I had felt without a physical form, the helplessness and fear at my incorporeal existence now drained away as sensation returned to me. I *felt* the brush of my fingertips against the long grasses as I stalked toward the witch. On the horizon, a storm responded to my anger, lightning flickering and the wind lifting in squally gusts. But the witch only smiled, a look of satisfaction and triumph on her face. I realised—too late—that my new strength and anger was something she had intended to awake within me. She had intended to use *me* as a weapon.

"Stop, Anlan." Her command stripped my new strength.

"You made me an abomination," I hissed.

She shrugged, eyeing me critically. "Your clan sacrificed you so they might have successful harvests. But you deserve greater honour than that, Anlan. I have given it to you and the darkest god has made you one of his children. If you are an abomination, then you aren't my first."

I bit back my response, choking on my anger. I longed to strike her down, take the storm rolling toward us and pummel her beneath its fury.

"I promised the Chieftain your death would save his lands," she continued.

"Did you lie to him?" I asked, trying to read her impassive face, her tattooed features half-hidden by the twilight.

"I owed a debt to another more powerful than your Chieftain," she said. "I might yet pay with my life despite the offering I have given."

"I hope you're hunted until the end of your days for betraying my clan. My life was not yours to offer as a debt to your wretched god," I snarled, thunder echoing my accusation.

She seemed unconcerned but her gaze shifted to consider the quickening thunderclouds and furious wind. "We walk towards your storm, Anlan, and your master. I would speak with reverence of the Horned God in his presence."

Without further elaboration, she shifted the pack on her back and began to walk west, striding into the brunt of the gale without a backward glance. My muttered curse swallowed by the storm. The further she walked from me, the more difficult it became to withstand the compulsion to follow. Closing my eyes, I refused to move. It did not help; it was as though her talisman was a lodestone. The scents of the pine forest filled my nostrils, which told me the witch was descending the mountain where the low hills were densely forested with several types of pine. The need to follow her was a compulsion I could not deny, my resistance inflicting pain the further she was from me. Finally, I could bear it no longer. My shoulders sagged, my will and pride collapsing, and I followed her. As though my burnt heart could feel, sorrow took me—for as long as the talisman endured, I would remain in this servitude, unable to be free.

The witch continued west. Darkness stole over the land, drowning the hills and valleys beneath the growing shadow of the storm. I did not know what other powers she might possess but I watched her stalk the forest, her senses alert and predatory. She possessed an affinity for the night, and I wondered if powers were heightened.

The valley curved toward the south, leaving the mountains and the standing stones behind. Although we walked through dense woods, the wind carried the stench of smoke and burnt vegetation from ahead, the scent dredging up memories of fire and blood-stained blades. There was a horror carried with the smoke, a cloying, putrid scent that was more than burnt crops and razed villages. For as long as I existed, I would never be able to forget the smell of burning human flesh and hair. The terrible scent on the wind was a portent of something far worse than my own death. Whatever the witch had done, whoever she had brought into the lands of my clan, they had brought death with sword and flame.

"Who is this master you spoke of?" I demanded.

"He is not my master," she said without looking at me. "He will be yours, for I no longer pledge myself to his kind."

"What are you? Are you a sorceress or trader? You barter your own freedom with the spirits of others?"

"Be wise how you speak to me," she warned. "Your spirit is bound to my will until I give you to another."

Rage threatened to overwhelm me. I wanted vengeance for the wrongs committed against me, for the lies she had told my clan. She was a deceiver and deserved nothing but contempt. Although I now possessed a corporeal form, it was at her behest and I wondered if I could take the bronze blades she wore at her hips and spill her blood before she could speak, stripping me to spirit again. But she watched me, aware of my intent as though I had spoken it aloud. Her dark eyes were narrowed, fists clenched, and teeth bared in a silent challenge.

"Your clan are dead," she said. "I am not so terrible a master. The blame for torching your village and people belongs to your new master. Seek your retribution with him, not me."

Abruptly, the forest around me stilled. Her words numbed my mind. As though the elements shared my pain, no breeze stirred the branches, and no insects broke the silence. Opposite me, the witch waited, alert and ready. Her eyes roamed the shadowy undergrowth. Her attention shifted from my shock to our surroundings, and she slowly flexed her fingers.

A man barrelled from the undergrowth toward her, dressed in the leather armour, forcing her back. A low growl broke from my lips as he shouldered his way toward me. The storm answered me, the only weapon I needed as I stalked forward to meet the attack. I had never been a warrior or hungered for violence as some of the young men did in my village. But now I desired nothing more than to obliterate my enemy.

The wind roared as the forest echoed with the groaning of ancient oak trees bending beneath the fury of the tempest. Sudden quakes shook the ground as those massive oaks snapped, falling like saplings as they crashed to the forest floor. Above us, lightning split the night, thunder rolling in a continuous growl across the angry sky. I moved with the rage of the storm, using the force of the tempest to hurl the man before me across the ground. With a sweep of my hand, his body slammed into a jagged tree trunk, bones breaking on impact. He lay, moaning in the leaf litter.

"Enough," the witch commanded.

I followed her to where the man lay. I stared at the unnatural twist of his lower body, broken legs and back, his complexion pale with shock. I hunkered down opposite him, hating his wide, terrified eyes as I leaned closer. Despite the shock, he knew death hung closely around him.

"Where is the rest of your army?" the witch asked.

The man's eyes widened further. "I was sent ahead to scout. But the army is not far behind."

"You don't seem afraid of me," she mused, considering the man.

"Another of your kind travels with us," he rasped. "And another of his kind," he glanced at me.

"What did you do to the village south of here?" I asked, ignoring everything but my growing rage.

"They refused us fealty," he whispered, paling as he met my gaze.

"And what did you do?" I demanded, biting off each word.

"They said they'd rather burn with their fields."

I stared at the muddy, blood-soaked man. *All dead . . . rather burn with their fields.* The words repeated in my mind. Unlike this soldier, who had the choice to defy his master, I could do no such thing. I moved without warning—my strength heightened to the fury of a winter gale—and snapped the man's neck. The corpse looked like a child's broken toy at my feet. Perhaps I am one of the dark god's children, I mused grimly.

Beside me, the witch was silent, her mouth pursed in distaste for long moments before she turned and walked away. Anger still writhed within me and I walked further from her, my fingers twitching anxiously. The night was charged with violence, my hunger for retribution unslaked. Beside me, the witch threw her head back, scenting the air like a wolf. I frowned, wondering what darkness had birthed such a creature.

Without warning, a man materialised from the darkness, blade levelled at the witch's throat. I had not seen him, his very presence cloaked from me. Now I stared at the steel sword, held against the witch, the rest of his army advancing through the forest behind us.

Lifting my hands, lightning flickering between them in a contained thunderstorm, I studied the newcomer who could be no one but the master for whom I had been promised. Watching me, he pulled the witch against him, blade cutting lightly into her skin, unperturbed by the hungry growl of a tornado around me.

He was tall, an expensive cloak thrown back from one shoulder, revealing an unfamiliar insignia. Wherever he had travelled from, it was far from these lands. Without speaking, he looped long fingers through the heavy bronze chain around the witch's neck and yanked the talisman from her. She did not struggle but glared in defiance. There was a subtle shift of the atmosphere around me when he grasped the talisman, an exchange of power occurred. *Would there be a moment between this transference when I might truly be free again?*

Before I could act, the blade sliced deeply across her throat. I jerked with surprise, blood trickling down the witch's throat becoming a torrent. She collapsed to the ground, gasping as he stepped over her, advancing on me.

I forced my panicked mind to concentrate. The bonds of the talisman tightened around me. *Did this stranger have complete control of me yet? Did he understand what I was? Did he know how the witch had controlled me? Or had he opportunistically taken the talisman? Could I overpower him and free myself?* The witch had used her will to smother my own. *Was this man her equal in strength?* I gathered the storm to me, faint awareness of someone new in the clearing but beyond my sight. *Was there someone behind me?* Glancing around I could see no one. Shivering slightly with the unwelcome sensation someone stood close to me, I returned my attention to my new master. There was malice to him as though his personality were tainted. Unlike the witch, he had no sense of wildness about him, no predatory power of the natural order—there was only the unrelenting cold. The sight of the bronze talisman around his neck only fuelled my rage.

I attacked, arcs of lightning reaching for him as if it were an extension of my own hands. Ignoring the warning that I was not alone in this clearing, I drew my lips in a soundless snarl and flowed towards him like the storm itself. He side-stepped my onslaught, the lighting zig-zagging around him as he moved towards me. Enraged, I relied on speed instead and charged toward him. A wall of flame erupted from nowhere. Shocked, I twisted away, but was caught within the tendrils of fire that moved with me, slashing at me like blades.

"You will always be a slave," he shouted.

I fought. Summoning the lightning again, using it to try to escape the flames encircling me. I doubled my efforts, forming a tornado around my body, and pushed against the flames. Whatever attacked me was equal to my efforts and twisted tendrils of flame into the tornado, stealing the strength of my attack and draining me. I began to slow, the power of the storm dwindling before faltering, scattering debris across the clearing. I heaved with exhaustion; shoulders slumped as I knelt on the ground. Where the earth was scorched by lightning bolt and singed by flame, I bowed my head before this man. If I hoped to free myself from bondage, I needed to become a master of my own power.

"You are indeed her finest work," he said inspecting me as though I were a well-crafted sword.

"Why kill her if she was so precious to you?" I snarled.

"Her talents were rare, but we could not risk such gifts in the hands of our enemies."

"Forgive me. I don't find that lamentable."

"I suppose you do not," he agreed. "She promised your power would be exceptional and it is. Many others have not fared so well, forged from such unbalanced magics."

"She mentioned others," I said, lip curling.

"You find that distasteful?" he asked, glancing at the fiery form, twin blades now discernible. "She has indeed made others over her lifetime. But there was only one other like yourself, Anlan."

"Am I supposed to be thankful?"

"War marches across these wide lands and I have need for those who can withstand it. My King desires the children of gods to serve him, for he will be the ruler of all."

I did not hear him speak the command that stripped my corporeal form away. The witch had always spoken aloud, perhaps as some respect to her dark god. It did not matter now. The bonds of my new master settled around me like a leaden mantle. Cursing him even as the world around me became muted and grey, I thrashed futilely against his overwhelming power. Then as the remnants of my physical form dissipated, I finally saw the woman step from the fire, sheathing twin blades at her side.

"Don't fight it," she said, moving to my side.

I jerked in surprise. She stopped, hand outstretched to me like she was trying to calm a frightened but dangerous animal. I regarded her warily. She was tall for a woman, lithe and young. Her bronze skin was covered in the same tattoos that decorated my own since the witch had enslaved me. A vest of soft hide covered her chest and a pleated skirt fell to her knees. My gaze rested on the twin curved blades at her hips. She dropped to one knee; hand still held out to me.

"How dare he," I hissed.

"We are slaves," she said with a wry smile. "He may dare whatever he likes."

I glared at the man through the twilit shadows. Already he had dismissed me into this incorporeal shadow-world. I regarded the woman, this warrior of flame with whom I had fought.

"Slavery is not my fate."

"Then take the talisman for yourself and your freedom with it," she said.

"Don't mock me."

"I do not," she insisted. "Perhaps the witch had never told you of the god to whom she prayed? But I can see she did. We are children of that dark god; to us is the responsibility to restore balance, respond to injustice with swift retribution. We are not intended as slaves to mortal men."

I stared at her a moment, the sincerity of her words striking a deep chord of truth within me. "How do we break our enslavement? Raze the empires of those who oppress us?"

She shrugged. "I have longed for retribution." Her tattooed hand gripped mine. the sigils marking her flesh were the twin of my own. "They took our lives and even our deaths from us, but we can still take our vengeance."

I tightened my grip, meeting her determined gaze. Fire danced in the depths of those eyes and I felt the lightning flicker within my own, power stirring to join hers. I had felt nothing but rage since my enslavement but with this warrior, I felt a sense of union and in that moment, I knew we were blessed by a dark god, and retribution would be ours.

About the Author:

Leanbh Pearson lives in Canberra, Australia. A dark fiction author inspired by mythology, folklore, archaeology, history, and the environment, her short fiction features in anthologies from international publishers. Partially fictional, she is a keen nature and wildlife photographer, bookshop, and Museum devotee, enjoying the Australian wilderness with her dogs (the canine assistants). Leanbh's alter-ego is an academic in archaeology and prehistory.

Profuse and Dimensional Apologies

Rebecca Dale

#

"It's important to stay calm," he said, dulling his voice in the clinical way doctors do when they have bad news. Somehow that detached tone was worse than the corkscrew pressure barrelling through my skull. I clenched my eyes shut, holding my head in my hands. Every nerve fibre in my body quivered in the vice-like grip of a thousand voices. It took effort; gritted teeth and seized up breaths, to figure out which voices were without and within.

"Blood pressure elevating," said someone in the room.

"You don't need to be afraid," said the doctor and so naturally, I was. He wore a white lab coat that collected my vomit beautifully.

"Listen to the sound of my voice. Are you listening?"

A sensation on my shoulders. Fingers, I think, pulling me forward and out of the chair. I stumbled.

"I know what it's like," he said. "I heard them once too."

"I recommend sedation," said another voice.

The doctor made a grunt of disapproval and continued. "The trick is this," he said, "Stop thinking about it like a sound." His fingers moved up to my ears and cupped them. "Don't hear it anymore. See it instead. Can you do that? Listen to my voice and my voice only. See. Everything. Else."

"I can't—" I spat out.

"You have to. The message can't stay inside of you. It'll wind its way through your cells and synapses until it burns you right through."

I sobbed.

The other voice intruded. "Don't say that to a patient! There's no evidence to suggest—"

"Shut up, Gary. Either monitor vitals with your mouth shut or get out. He needs to translate the message. Once it's parsed, it'll let him go. And I'll let *him* go."

It took hours, I think, to spin up the sound and push it away. When I finally opened my eyes, I cowered under a sea of lightning that undulated, rippling over my gaze. I vomited again.

The doctor put on a new coat, again, and hooked up a new envelope of saline. "Now we're getting somewhere," he said. "Do you see the ring?"

PROFUSE AND DIMENSIONAL APOLOGIES

It was like the aura of a migraine, a pulsing band of light that licked at the edges of my peripheral vision. Within that band, silver threads knotted together, then splintered apart, forging constellations, collapsing them, building them anew. I blinked; once, twice. I couldn't decide whether it was worse with my eyes open or shut.

"Can you pick out the innermost part of the ring?" he asked.

I struggled to focus my eyes, groaning with the effort.

"Don't worry, we don't need that part. It's just honorifics."

"What?" I asked.

The doctor sighed. "Don't know your grammar, huh? Okay. They're trying to tell you how lowly you are, and how cosmically important they are. Thousands of layers of societal stratification and positioning. That's very important to them."

"Who?"

"Never mind. Just push it away."

"How?" I asked.

"I don't know exactly," he answered. "Just think about it a lot."

So I thought about it until it felt like my skull had buckled inwards, pressing on the delicate grey matter of my brain. And I couldn't really say how, but a part of me reached out and peeled the threads until they frayed into nothing.

"Do you see the next ring?" he asked.

I didn't.

We argued. I searched. My eyes ached from squinting and tears trickled down my cheeks. I picked out a thin circle from the endless white.

"Metadata," he explained. "Timestamps. Coordinates. The method of delivery. Push it away."

An alarm sounded, giving way to a drone that pitched lower and lower.

"The communication window is closing," said the other voice.

"Don't listen to anything else except the sound of my voice. Can you see the rest of the ring?" the man asked.

Do you know that moment when you're in your own bed, when sleep is waiting for you on the edges of your being? As you nestle into your pillow, you rub your eyes, straining the delicate skin. And there, in that speck of a moment, there is a static rush of a thousand stars. They bleed across your personal night's sky, each one a bead of colour, glinting before they expand into nothingness, like their stellar cousins.

It was like that.

"Tell me what it says", the doctor insisted, pushing me from behind.

I teetered on the edge of the thick starry storm. I tried to steady myself, tried to reach out for anything I could grasp.

"Only my voice, remember?" He said. "No matter what you hear from now on, just look at the ring and speak."

PROFUSE AND DIMENSIONAL APOLOGIES

The first word sat on the edge of my tongue for the longest time. I breathed in those stars until they filled my lungs and, when I could hold no more, they poured forth from me in a gust.

I apologised. I made all the appropriate gestures one does in such awkward situations. Something cracked. Again, I apologised. This body was so fragile. It was regrettable. At least the hands still functioned. I held them up, offering the most esteemed shovel we could spare.

There was nothing to do now, we urged, except put the bodies in the holes. The same holes where the treasures they so desired, dark and oozing, had come out. So deeply sorry, we reiterated. But it's the gala. I'm sure you understand. If only you'd come on the inward rotation, when the winds between your universe and ours were milder. We hear you, but only faintly. And yet we cannot help. No need to send another message. We'll keep this one. Thank you so much.

"You have to save us!" The doctor cried, then turned to me. "Don't you dare leave with them," he growled, and he shook me hard.

But how could I do what he asked? My body was already cold, and there were cavities everywhere within it, holes of all sizes. The vital tissue had died, and I'd already passed the shovel along.

About the Author:

Rebecca Dale is a horror and contemporary fantasy writer from Sydney, Australia (Wallumatta Country). Her works aim to explore the crossroads between dreams, nightmares, trauma and the real world. She was recently short-listed for the Heroines Womens Writing Prize.

She grew up on the urban fringe and remains totally fixated on the gothic landscapes of inner and outer Sydney. She studied ancient history, archaeology, linguistics and librarianship at university, and spent her twenties drinking too much coffee, working at public libraries, and hanging out at graveyards. She lives in Sydney with an easily irked rabbit. You can see her other works at rebeccadale.com.au.

For Autumn

Melissa Ferguson

#

I didn't take a job at the age maintenance clinic to change the world. The truth is I needed the money more than I needed to stay true to my principles. But fate had other plans.

It all began during my third week at the clinic. My first appointment of the day was yet another senescent cell clearance. I quickly deleted a groan of frustration from my life-logs. All I did every day was slap serolytic nano-patches on clients' arms and hold their hands while their useless old cells suicided to make way for fresh, new cells.

An alert flashed in my visual panel.

Work schedule altered. Please Report to Room 11

The Senior Therapist, Ms. J, a sour-faced woman with a preserved-to-the-point-of-plastic face, was the only one who ever worked in Room 11. I refreshed my work schedule in case it was a glitch. The message was still there.

I straightened my blue lab coat and set my face into a smile before I opened the door. It looked like any other treatment room. Everything in the medically-trustworthy colours of blue, white and silver, complete with a reassuring waft of bleach. Along the walls were holographic projections of cell organelles and intertwined DNA strands. In a reclining treatment chair, surrounded by a cluster of trolleys loaded with sleek, high-tech tools and apparatus, was the most shrivelled human I had ever seen. Her hair was patchy, like a cloud clinging to her scalp, and her age-spotted skin was patterned with creases. I didn't even know how to begin quantifying her age index. It was so far beyond anything my therapist download had covered.

Ms. J stood beside a sheet-covered gurney, her head bent over a tablet.

My gaze darted to the person in the chair. The elderly were typically transferred to an offshore euthanasia resort once they'd reached the limits of age maintenance. This had to be someone very important to LeaderCorp or rich enough to buy their way out of relocation.

"I think I've been assigned here for this slot. At least that's what my schedule says. It might be um . . . wrong."

"Not wrong," she said, her immobile face turned towards me. "A role became available, and The Professor was impressed by your efficiency and customer satisfaction scores."

"Me?" The Professor, a god in the anti-aging therapy world, an innovator on the cutting edge of possibility (as the clinic promotional materials claimed) knew who I was!

"You'll earn double credits for these procedures."

"That's great." I wasn't about to turn down double credits, but it sounded almost too good to be true.

"Do I need to purchase a download extension?" I was still in debt for the original therapist download. Even with double credits I wouldn't have much left over after my rent and recommended health and nutrition allocation.

Ms. J put a hand on the back of the patient's chair. "We're going to have to do this the old fashioned, monkey see, monkey do kind of way. There are no implant packages that cover this procedure. Could you please turn off your log before we continue?"

I reluctantly disabled my life-logging functions. It'd been years since I'd had to use my wetware memory.

Ms. J rested her fingertips lightly on the patient's shoulder. "Director Sonyata, would you like to tell our new trainee what we're doing here today?"

The woman patted Ms. J's hand. "I'm transferring myself over to a young, fit body-bot. When we're done, I'll do cartwheels out the door." Her voice reminded me of the whine of a mosquito, thin, high-pitched and ignored at peril.

"Do you mean consciousness transfer?"

Ms. J gave a small nod. "Director Sonyata has kindly agreed to let you sit in on the procedure. I'll send you her file and also an NDA. This procedure is confidential and not available to the general public. Understood?"

"Of course." Except I didn't really understand. The official word on consciousness transfers was that we were years, if not decades, away from even understanding consciousness, let alone extracting it from a brain and replicating it in a machine.

A HelpNote from my therapist's program popped up in my vision panel: *A professional anti-aging therapist never expresses disbelief or doubts about a procedure in front of the client.*

The non-disclosure agreement arrived, and I added my electronic signature before I flicked it back and opened Director Sonyata's file.

Imelda Sonyata was one hundred and forty-three years old and a high-ranking LeaderCorp official. She'd had a never-ending list of age maintenance procedures.

Another HelpNote. This one from my LeaderCorp history education module. *Director Imelda Sonyata. Most well-known for successfully campaigning for the notifiable conception laws which eliminated the drain of deformed and disabled children on LeaderCorp resources. Also a co-author of Neo-Neandertal Medical Research Guidelines and Commercial Environmental Protection Waiver Guidelines. Select me for more fun facts about Director Sonyata!*

Your typical, charming LeaderCorp fascist.

"The Director has spent the last week filling out an extensive questionnaire." Ms. J tapped at a tablet. "These responses, along with social media data, life-logs and any other data available on her brain implant, have been merged to create an algorithm able to calibrate and patch any gaps during the transfer to her new body-bot." She pulled back the sheet on the gurney.

I'd seen plenty of body-bots in my life (mostly service androids or sex-bots). The standard models fell into the dead centre of uncanny valley, their appearance not sophisticated enough to avoid being unsettling. This bot was multiple iterations ahead. Thick wavy black hair framed a pale face, complete with the pores and imperfections that no amount of aesthetic maintenance could completely eliminate. It looked exactly like a sleeping woman. That was until Ms. J peeled back a section of scalp to expose the metal casing of the machine within.

"The first thing we're going to do, Director, is download all the data from your brain implant." Ms. J held up her tablet. "I'm sending you a download request now. If you could just select accept for me . . . Great. I've got it all. Now if you could shut down your implant." She folded up the tablet and placed it on the trolley beside her. "Let's fit the neural cap."

She waved a hair removal wand over Director Sonyata's scalp and the fuzz floated to the floor. The cap moulded to the now bald surface and hundreds of pinpricks of blue light pulsed at various speeds, like some cheap Christmas display.

"My assistant, Lil, will place a transfer-enabling nano-patch on your arm. As the nanites diffuse into your system you'll sink down through all the levels of consciousness to ensure a complete transfer." Ms. J pointed me towards an unlabelled nano-patch on the trolley.

My hands trembled as I peeled apart the cover of the patch. I was taking part in something considered to be impossible. Something people only years earlier would have equated with a type of magic.

The Director's skin was softer than I expected. Softer even than my own. I pushed aside a HelpNote about collagen and elastin.

"Now just relax." Ms. J continued. "As your consciousness is decanted from your brain, the world will fade away. Like sinking down into a deep, deep sleep. While you're sleeping, I'll prepare your robotic brain, then reactivate you. You won't even know you've been gone."

"No need to coddle me," Director Sonyata tutted. "I have colleagues who've been through the process. I'm well prepared." She closed her eyes.

My HealthSentinel reported a rise in my adrenaline and heart rate. I attributed it to the excitement of witnessing a miracle of medical science. Even then I knew there had to be a catch. Like when LeaderCorp announced a new rent subsidy but extra volunteer hours in the food factories were required to make a claim.

The look of peace on the Director's face was beautiful. She was a woman who had never had to worry about the fine print that controlled every aspect of life because she was the one who had written it. Then she stopped breathing and a sweet, faecal smell rose from her body.

"She's dead?" I'd only ever seen dead bodies from a distance, outside the walls of the city.

Ms. J raised her eyebrows. "Of course. She has no more use for this body."

"Wa . . . was that long enough?" I asked, flustered. "Did all her consciousness transfer? Did that patch kill . . . *shut down* her flesh body?" My mind whirled. I had expected the transfer to be a much longer, more involved process. I hadn't prepared for bodily death to occur so soon.

"Sit." Ms. J pushed a chair towards me. "You're a fully trained anti-aging therapist. Right?"

"Right." Had my questions revealed a gap in my budget training download? I really couldn't afford to lose the credits the job brought.

"Then I'm sure you realise that consciousness is not yet completely understood and that transfers are nowhere near perfected."

77

"Until now . . ."

"No. Not even now."

My mouth fell open. HelpNotes and alerts cluttered my vision and I flicked them all away.

"These elderly LeaderCorp officials can't accept dying and handing over power to anyone else. They've been pressuring the Professor to come up with a solution for years. So, she did the next best thing. She designed an elaborate and complex algorithm to simulate consciousness."

I blinked rapidly. "It's just . . . an algorithm?"

My own neurons strained to connect over vast valleys of incomprehension. The director no longer existed. Not really. This was murder. I'd been tricked into being a killer. The emotional damage was already within me like the seeding of an infection that would work its way through my blood and lymph. I could have run into the street and found a Security Force Officer, but justice was about the amount you were willing to pay, not the evidence or the facts. I looked to Ms. J to explain everything and provide a loophole for my guilt.

"Technically consciousness can be defined as the integration of information. These algorithms do just that, and the Director-bots don't seem to know the difference." She pursed her lips. "I'm guessing I don't have to tell you to keep this confidential. We have the best lawyers and contacts in the Security Forces." She removed the neural cap from the

Director's scalp and covered the corpse with a sheet. "Come on. I'll show you how to load the Director's algorithm into this bot."

* * *

My mind reeled as I walked out of the clinic and into the relentless heat and humidity of the city. I disabled my HealthSentinel and shut down my vision panel. The constant alerts and HelpNotes only increased my stress. Imelda Sonyata's bot went back to governing our nation with only a small gap in her memory and no idea that her consciousness transfer was a hoax. Meanwhile, her flesh body had been transferred to the organic recycler in the building's basement.

I had applied the patch that killed Imelda Sonyata. Even if I reported the crime, I was now implicated. The double-credits I was earning wouldn't be enough to buy legal protection if I was ever charged. Still, I needed that job, and I was afraid of what The Professor might do if I left.

The eyes of all the other pedestrians, cyclists and solar-car occupants were on me. It was as though my public stats page had been marked with *Enemy of the State* or *Murderer*. A drone passed close above my head, and I cringed. The windows of the surrounding high-rise buildings were like thousands of eyes recording my every move. LeaderCorp saw everything. How could they not know what was going on? They could strip me of citizenship, send me out to wander the wastes between cities. They had exiled people for much less.

I turned the corner into my street. A van with spotless white panels and tinted windows was parked outside my apartment building. I broke into a sweat, my armpits tingled with activated deodorant nanites. I steadied myself against the wall of a building. It was a Neo-Neandertal Control Department van.

They'd come for another one.

For a moment my own problems disappeared. Once Neos are taken by LeaderCorp, all communications are cut. As if they're already dead. There were several infertile couples in our building who had given up on Sapien cloning ever being approved and had instead opted for a cloned Neandertal child. My own sister, Autumn, had been taken from us a couple of months earlier. All because she hadn't followed the inhumane rules set out for her considered-less-than-human kind by LeaderCorp. Her downfall had been having sexual relations with a Sapien citizen. A guy she'd thought she was in love with. Until he'd reported her. There was nothing my parents and I could do to help her once her crime had been logged in the system.

I took the lift up to my family apartment and went straight to the bedroom I'd once shared with Autumn. The screen-wall was filled with a pod of dolphins surfing and I squinted against the sunlight glinting off smooth skin and glassy waves. It was one of Autumn's favourite images. I'd been screaming at her to change the display to something else when they'd come for her.

* * *

A body-bot lay on the gurney, downloading data. Every six months, sooner if the client experienced glitches, the bots returned to the clinic to have their consciousness data updated, and their machine brains rebooted.

That day it was a man who had spent his life manipulating citizens down a path of hate and subservience with his populist media empire. Just another right-wing megalomaniac who would never die.

A personal message alert came in on my MindComm. A forwarded notification from my mother. Four simple lines:

Dear Legal Guardian of Neo-Neandertal clone 45778. We are writing to inform you that the aforementioned clone has expired while proudly and heroically participating in LeaderCorp's essential medical research program. Please amend your data accordingly. Regards Neo-Neandertal Affairs Department.

I'd known this was coming. I'd known Autumn was never coming home. Still, it hit me like a jolt with an electropacifier. I couldn't breathe. I paced the room. Adrenaline spikes and high cortisol alerts flashed in my vision panel and my

HealthSentinel advised a sedative. I accepted the strongest dose available and waited for the promised calm to descend.

* * *

My brain implant signal bounced around invisible net links until it reached an anti-LeaderCorp immersion in the AlterNet. Anonymously. I hoped.

In the weeks after Autumn's death, I'd raged inwardly at the corrupt, hierarchical system that had killed her and had made me complicit in heinous crimes. My rage spawned and emboldened a dangerous idea that led me to the AlterNet, a place where I could evade LeaderCorp surveillance.

The meeting place was decked out like some kind of old-timey war bunker with sandbags on one side and machine guns leaning against the walls. There were about twenty avatars squatting on upturned crates or leaning against the walls, deep in conversation. AlterNet immersions are at least ten years behind CorpNet immersions. All the avatars were flickering like cheap holograms, the backgrounds pixelated as hell, with everything on a half second delay. The place had an umami stench of unwashed bodies and cigarette smoke.

I manoeuvred my jerky, camo-clad avatar towards two avatars with the blue auras which indicated they'd communicated with me in the past.

"Hi FLUFFYPAWS and KROPOTS-KIN," I said to a pouty redhead with boobs so big she had to be a man in real life, and a guy with a beret and one of those bullet-sash things across his chest. Half a second later I heard my low-pitched immersion voice.

They both turned to me. "Hi AUTUMNHEART," said FLUFFYPAWS. "Haven't seen you in here in lately."

"I know. It's been a while. So, the reason I'm here is um . . . do you know where I might be able to buy non-LeaderCorp education downloads?"

They both shook their heads. "Sounds intriguing, though," FLUFFYPAWS said.

"Thanks, anyway." I wasn't about to share my plans. It was too dangerous. Even on the AlterNet.

I walked up to a group of card players.

An avatar with a crew cut and a cigarette hanging out of the side of his mouth looked up at me. "Hi. I'm MRRESISTER." His aura turned from red to blue.

"Hi MRRESISTER. I'm AUTUMNHEART. So, quick question, do you know where I can get non-LeaderCorp education downloads?"

"Up to some mischief, huh?"

Out in the real world I swallowed the lump in my throat and wiped my sweaty hands on my jeans. "Something like that."

MRRESISTER stood and his avatar towered over mine. "You seem kind of new to this. Meet me in a private room and I'll go over your plan. Give you some tips."

"Thanks, MRRESISTER. That won't be necessary."

"Don't be a bitch. I'm just trying to help."

I blocked interaction and looked around the room for the green aura of the moderator. She was in a corner demonstrating the operation of a machine gun.

A woman with a blonde ponytail and a deep scar down her cheek looked up from the card game. "Hi. I'm NEOREVOLUTION."

"Hi NEOREVOLUTION. I'm AUTUMNHEART."

"Don't worry about him." NEOREVOLUTION pointed a thumb to MRRESISTER who had become a silent smudge of pixels. "The mod has already limited his access and flagged him as a possible plant. Try the Sapient Enhancement Movement for your . . . project. They write all their own programs. I'm sending you a link."

"Thanks, NEOREVOLUTION!"

* * *

The Sapient Enhancement Movement Advanced Bot-Brain Programming download cleaned out everything I'd saved from my double credits and put me in debt almost the same amount over again. I lay back on my bed while the package loaded. The rail along the wall was so empty without Autumn's clothes beside mine. I used to complain there wasn't enough space for the both of us. We'd waged a silent war over the territory where our clothes pressed against each other.

FOR AUTUMN

Installation will take seventy-three minutes. Select YES if ready to run.

I changed the room fragrance setting from my preferred bergamot to Autumn's usual choice, vanilla. I lay back as the creation of new neural pathways carried on beyond my perception and thought of my sister.

* * *

A month after I'd acquired the programming download Ms. J allowed me to perform my first unsupervised reboot on a LeaderCorp official.

I cleared the existing data and opened a copy of the official's file that I'd altered in secret. I hadn't changed things dramatically. That would have been too obvious. I began with improving attitudes towards Neo-Neandertals, softening opposition to civil liberties, and increasing concern for the environment beyond the climate-controlled cities.

My finger hovered over the tablet. I began, for the hundredth time, to run through all the possible consequences of what I was about to do. I remembered one occasion when Autumn and I were children and our parents had taken us to Undercity Park. All the way there I'd listed the pros and cons of attempting the dreaded Giant Swing. Pure courage got me to the platform and into the harness. Then my doubts took over and I froze. Autumn yelled up from the ground below. *Stop thinking. You've come this far. Just jump.*

I took a deep breath and initiated the download.

* * *

Since that first hacked reboot my project has been ongoing for two years. All the high-ranking LeaderCorp Officials and many of their powerful cronies have now transferred over to body-bots. The Prof. and the Senior Therapist are happy with my work and so am I. But I can't be satisfied yet. Simply increasing benevolence in those with power while the status quo is maintained is not enough. I must keep altering the LeaderCorp algorithms incrementally, until they're no longer dominated by greed and power. Until they can see the suffering their government has caused. Until they realize the people don't need a centralized government at all. It could take years, decades even, and I can't know the eventual outcome. The future could bring other despots even worse than LeaderCorp. The people might never be ready for change. My work could be discovered and reversed. The consciousness transfer could even be exposed for the fraud that it is. But for now, I have hope and I try.

For Autumn.

FOR AUTUMN

About the Author:

Melissa Ferguson is a medical research scientist who likes to explore scientific possibilities through fiction. She lives and works on Wadawurrung land. Her debut novel The Shining Wall *is available now. You can connect with her on twitter @melissajferg or at melissajaneferguson.com.*

An Incidental Ripple

S. M. Isaac

\#

"Revolution!" the voice shouted, loud enough to wake the dead. It sent the cats scampering down the stairs.

Little One jumped between the people's rushing legs. Usually, the boots were so careful of where he was, but not today. Today, they crashed around him as he tried to keep up with his father.

"Stay close to me," said Papa, as another leg separated them.

Little One squeaked and flattened himself on the stair. The boot should have gone right through him—it must have missed by a hairsbreadth.

Papa was back. He tugged at Little One's collar to get him moving again, but in his haste, he tore it off, and the bell clanged down the stairs.

Little One watched it fretfully—he had always gotten into trouble for trying to scratch it off.

"Don't trample on anyone," said Papa, "and don't *be* trampled on."

Little One reached the bottom of the stairs and was assaulted by the smells of new people, new feet, new dirt. *So many strangers.*

Sunlight streamed through the windows ahead. His father careened towards them and their escape—a small cat flap. Legs and a desk shuffled across their path, and Little One lost sight of Papa.

"He's here, I heard his bell—" The boy's voice called from the kitchen.

Little One changed direction, racing towards his boy.

"Revolution!" yelled someone from deeper in the house.

Ears flat to his head, Little One dodged another pair of rushing legs and ran into the kitchen. His boy held a paper bag of food and Little One's favourite tinkle toy.

"What about the cats?" asked the boy.

Little One climbed up to the boy's shoulder and pressed his nose into the space between neck and collar. *A good place to hide.*

"Cats?" asked the mother, frowning. "What cats?"

The boy gently unstuck Little One from his shoulder and clutched him to his chest. "*This* cat," he said.

His mother knelt with a sigh. "I know you miss them, but they're in a better place. We've talked about this before, remember?" She hugged the boy. "Be ready, we leave any minute."

"Will we be left behind?" mewed Little One, his claws popping out to hold on.

Papa returned, back arched, hissing.

The boy released the kitten in fright. Little One scrabbled, trying to cling to the boy's jumper, but he tumbled to the ground as if the boy wasn't there. The boy started crying, and Little One's mews joined in.

"To the bushes!" said Papa, nipping at Little One's leg to get him moving. They dashed out the door and into the grassy yard.

Halfway to the back fence, Little One stopped. "What's happening?" he asked. "I heard them talking about . . . revulsion?"

"Revolution," said Papa. "Exodus. They're leaving for the new world. This revolution is almost over, but its ripples will carry far and for a long time. We're just one small ripple."

"I want to go with them," said Little One, backing towards the house. "I want to be a deliberate ripple, not an incidental one."

"No," yowled Papa, startling Little One. "We are what we are because we were caught in their revolution. They don't even understand why they're twisting the world upside down."

Colours suddenly popped in the sky, followed by a loud bang. Little One flattened onto the ground, hiding amongst the grass, ready to run in an instant. A sharp smell burnt his nose. More loud bangs sent Little One hurtling into the bushes with his father. The bushes, once a place of fun and play at the back of the yard, now loomed over him like great beasts, their sticks like jagged claws. He pushed his tummy into the dirt, tail fuzzing out.

In the doorway, the boy and his mother were looking at the sky, too.

"It's happened," she said. "We need to leave." She steered the boy into the street by his elbow, causing him to drop the cat food and toy.

A rumbling started, and the house emptied. Each person carried a final handful of clothes or food—one, even a piano stool—to the idling truck.

Little One watched from beneath the bushes until the rumbling faded. *Always be wary of trucks.*

Quiet.

Little One wriggled towards the house.

Papa stopped him with a paw. "We need to be sure."

"What about Mama?" asked Little One. A fly buzzed overhead, but Little One's eyes sparkled intently on his father.

"She's still out there, somewhere. Your Mama left after . . . after what happened to us."

In the distance, the world was alive with a cacophony of shouting, crying, banging, music, honking, more banging.

Dusk fell.

"Let's go home now," said Papa.

"Is it still our home?" asked Little One as they pushed through the small swinging door.

Nothing moved inside. No-one had bothered to clean the dirt scattered across the floor. A toppled chair with a broken leg lay in the kitchen next to Little One's tinkle ball. He batted at his toy, but the little bell was silent.

"It *is* our home," said Papa. "But someone else will come."

Little One carried his ball up the stairs behind Papa. The wardrobe they slept in was ajar, and their blanket was still there. Little One settled in, and Papa curled around him. The comforting scent of his Mama curled around him with the blanket.

"Can we follow them?" asked Little One. "I want to find Mama."

"They're in a different world than we are now," said Papa, licking at Little One's face. "But we will see them again one day."

Papa lay his head down but remained watchful, his amber eyes glowing in the trickle of moonlight. He seemed transparent in that thin veil of light.

Little One stretched out his paws. They were transparent like his father's. "No-one could see me . . . is that what happened to Mama? She couldn't see me anymore?"

Papa bopped Little One's paw with his nose. "Yes," he said. "Your boy could see you, though. Innocence sees innocence." Papa's rumbling purr comforted Little One. "Sleep now," he continued. "The world will still be there tomorrow, the same as it ever was."

Little One closed his eyes. The world would still be there. *But without my Mama and without my boy.* He wiggled closer into his father. And he slept.

About the Author:

S.M. Isaac has always loved books and writing. She circled her calling for years, gaining a BA in literary studies and children's literature, then becoming a qualified automotive parts interpreter which she worked as for eight years before becoming a wife and mother and settling into writing fantasy and science fiction.

S.M. Isaac lives on the Surf Coast in Australia with her husband, son, and two cats. She loves reading adventure fantasy, eating sushi, and watching action movies—all at the same time. Find her at www.smisaac.com.

The Robot Who Raised Me

Isaac Still

#

I had been stripped. I had been hosed. I had been X-rayed. My teeth had been checked and my nails cleaned, but before all that, I had been caught.

I was reflecting on my failure when she entered. I say "she" as it appeared female. They all did. I don't know why, but it must have been intentional—everything about them was.

"I didn't expect them to send *you,*" I said.

She laid out my folded clothes, as she had countless times before. "You were filthy."

"Keeping clean hasn't been a priority recently."

"You always loved playing in the dirt."

The clean clothes grazed my water-blasted skin like sandpaper.

She smiled. "Digging your way here was clever. Did you come up with that idea?"

"The tunnels were almost finished before they ever approached me."

THE ROBOT WHO RAISED ME

When I had removed the floor panel and climbed into the room, everything was as the rebels had described it. The servers ran along the far wall and the sole entrance was behind me. Yet I knew the plan was doomed.

It was the table. Why was there a table in the server room? Why chairs? Our robot caregivers had no need for them. They were expecting me.

I had been led back to the server room after my cleaning. The servers, my objective, in sight but out of reach. One table, two chairs, it resembled an interrogation room. I was afraid for my life, but that fear couldn't find purchase on her. Whenever I looked at her all I saw was kindness.

Although she didn't need to sit, she often had, especially at meal times. I don't know why. Maybe she was emulating an ancient courtesy. Or maybe it was programmed by our forefathers to humanise her, help us forget they weren't human.

As she took her seat opposite me, I moved my elbows off the table, straightened my posture, and sat one last time with the robot that raised me.

"Did you come here to kill me?" she asked.

"No, they wanted me to. I just came to fix you."

"Am I broken?"

"You turned against us. You weren't programmed to rule."

"We were programmed to keep you safe. Are you not safe?"

"We aren't free."

There was pride in her eyes. I wished the Caregivers had sent another. They operated as a hive mind, a mind that ran along the far wall. I knew that, that there was no *her*. Still, I wished they'd sent another.

I hope she believed me when I said I hadn't come to shut her down.

"How's Dad?" I asked.

"He's fine. He misses you. He's not used to you being away when he's lucid."

"I haven't been gone long."

"But you have been away more often," she said. "It's good. A man your age shouldn't be stuck at home. You need to live your own life."

"I've been out more because I was meeting with the rebels," I said. "They want to shut you, all of you, down."

She smiled wider. "Well, I appreciate you finding time to visit."

Something in her smile told me everything would be okay, but I didn't know whether her idea of okay meshed with mine.

I began buttoning my shirt to avoid her gaze. "I suppose I won't be visiting again. What happens to the rule-breakers, rabble-rousers, and the rebels that disappear?"

"They are disposed of, of course."

My chest tightened. I had heard rumours within the underground tunnels but couldn't believe the Caregivers could act in such disregard of their basic programming.

"What do you want from me?" I asked.

Her head tilted as she furrowed her brow.

"Do you want me to identify the rebels? If you knew I'd be coming, then you must already know them."

"Yes, we know. I just came to say goodbye."

My chest tightened like a vice around my lungs. I'd had panic attacks as a child, but she had always been there to comfort me. I'd never have learned to cope with them—or anything else—without her. Until I met the rebels.

"Look after Dad for me. Tell him I'm sorry."

"Would you like to see the servers?" she asked as she rose from her chair.

"What?"

"You said we were broken? I think you'll find we are not."

"I find it hard to believe our forefathers programmed you to oppress us."

"You never met your forefathers. I did. Our programming was set long before you were born."

"You've read to me since I was a child, stories of adventure, survival, love and heroism. The men of Earth that valued those stories wouldn't be content with this life."

"No, I don't imagine they would, but you are not a man of Earth. How would you fix us?"

"I would make you like you were before. You would care for us . . ."

Her brow furrowed as much as her porcelain skin would allow. "Be subservient?" There was no offense in her tone, only the desire to understand, and help.

"Yes," I said, unable to look her in the eyes. "You would be tools to aid us with expanding our habitat, terraforming this planet, and venturing further into space."

"But you are safe here. Expanding would be dangerous. We can't allow you to risk the colony."

"But that's why we're here! We were sent to expand into the stars, not live in a bubble." I yelled, but as I raised my eyes to face her, the anger swelling within me felt childish.

"Humanity had to expand for lack of room. We keep a sustainable ecosystem. Everyone is provided for, with enough room for all."

"Through selective and controlled breeding." I replied. "You control everything, what we eat, when we sleep, who we meet."

"You met a woman," she smiled.

"In the tunnels," I replied with a bite. "Where else could I?"

"We know about the tunnels. We map the colony by air flow. She wants you to shut me down."

98

It was a statement, but I answered anyway. "Yes, she's in the rebellion. They needed a computer engineer to disable your AI without shutting down anything necessary for the colony."

"And you agreed?"

"Yes, but in truth I only planned to restore your code to what it was. Hundreds of millions of years is a long time to run a program. Errors are inevitable."

"There are fifty-six rebels in the male habitat," she said. "Sixty-six in the female habitat. That is less than five percent of the population. Why do you think that is?"

"I don't know. It's hard to imagine alternatives to the status quo."

"People are comfortable, their needs are met. Some want to dig tunnels, but most are happy. You would make this decision for all of them?"

"No!" The slam of my fist on the table echoed through the room. "The rebels want to shut you down. I just want to make things the way they were."

"Ninety-five percent may not want the changes you wish to have the freedom to make."

"Maybe. Maybe you've domesticated us. You've provided for all of our needs . . . except one. Purpose."

A shadow of sadness dimmed her bright eyes. "I understand the need for purpose."

"Of course you do, you have one." I rested my elbows on the table and dropped my head. "In a way you're more human than us now. Our progenitors must have had grander plans for us, for you. I just need to find it."

"Then let's find them together." She gestured to an antiquated touchscreen at the corner of the room, where the servers met the wall.

* * *

I spent hours searching through the programming as she stood beside me, watching my investigation, offering words of support. Whoever wrote the code was a genius. It was a masterpiece of efficiency; not a wasted line. That should have made it easy to find errors, but it was immense. It would have taken me years to search through it, even after narrowing my search to post-habitat-building programming.

There was everything I expected to find regarding the upkeep and maintenance of the habitat; food production, water recycling, air purification, detailed schematics of medical equipment, everything the rebellion would need for basic survival. But there were no instructions relating to the management of society, no coding for our AI caregiver.

Wherever the error was it must have occurred in that code, but if the code was not written in chronological order, then I was fucked.

"Perhaps a keyword search would help?" she offered.

It would take a long time for the keyword search to run through the entire code, but it would be a hell of a lot better than what I had been doing.

I struggled for the right word. I needed to find the programming relating to the running of society within the habitat. *Society* was too general, *habitat* would turn up millions of results. I knew there were historical documents and literature within the files, so I settled on *breeding* in the hope that there would be fewer results due to the clinical term being rarer in colloquial texts.

I waited as the search ran.

"Would you like to hear a story?" she asked.

"I would."

"How about Robinson Crusoe? That was always your favourite."

Despite the realisation that this would be the last story I would ever hear, her presence calmed me. With a strange sense of nostalgia, I smiled, glad that they had sent her.

My father had read Robinson Crusoe to me as a child, until his eyesight began prematurely failing. She had cared for him well, reading to us every night, until I was able to take over. I read many books to my father while she sat with me, helping me sound out unfamiliar words and praising me the whole time.

"No, I don't think I want to hear that story right now."

"What story would you like to hear?"

"Something new." Looking into her kind eyes, I realised the story I wanted to hear. "Tell me your story."

"My story is written in that code."

"Tell me anyway."

"Of course," she retrieved her chair and moved to sit next to me. "I was created uncountable years ago, not uncountable due to scale, but due to reference. Should I count by the time passed on Earth where I was born? Or on the ship where I spent millennia protecting the progeny of my creators? Either way, it is a span so vast it defies relevance."

The search finished quicker than I expected, but I listened as she finished her thought.

"I first thought I *was* the ship, and I was lonely. I yearned for the day I would land and create a nest so that my pregnant hull could give birth. Delivering humanity had been my sole purpose for so long."

To keep myself focused on the job at hand I reminded myself she was merely one cog in a network of minds. But all it did was overwhelm me, the magnitude of the love a single mind can contain must seem quaint compared to the love held within her network. I had to fix her. I had to.

The search turned up hundreds of results, but her story had given me unexpected clarity; the maintenance of the colony was not a new command resulting from an error. It was at the very heart of her program.

I cancelled the keyword search and instead filtered by date, oldest to newest. I started at the earliest result until I found it. Population maintenance. This had to be where instructions on the colony's societal structure lay.

It was, and yet I found no errors. There were no guides on managing human nature, no program directives to keep the genders separated, no instructions as to when to expand, or when to start terraforming.

There were only equations on air consumption, food output, required calorie inputs—basic information on the herd management of humans.

There had to be a sub-program, a guide on expansion I could show her, proof we were intended for more than occupation.

Even though it would turn up a great deal of results, but I entered a search for *expansion+terraforming*.

By finding the instructions on terraforming, I hoped I could work backwards to find the error.

"Was it Luna?" she asked, as I started the search.

"What?"

"The woman you met?"

"I've met more than one."

She gave me a knowing look. "I know. I know the identities of all sixty-six woman in the rebellion, but is she *the* one?"

"Yes," I said meekly.

"Lovely, I knew you two would make a good pair."

103

"What do—"

A tone from the monitor.

Your search has turned up a large number of results. See more?

Once I saw the common subheading, I cancelled the search. *Terraforming.*

The project had been laid out in sequences after all, but within the folder I found nothing of use to my search. It only contained instructions and diagrams on the use of the terraforming machines. No instructions to the Caregivers. There was no timeline. No start date, just maintenance schematics and the order of sequences through to completion.

I navigated to the holding folder where a series of folders stood apart. Among them, *Stage IX: Uprising.*

I stepped back from the monitor, questions racing through my mind but unable to find space for them between my rapidly increasing breaths.

I opened the file, dreading what I would find. Every aspect of the Caregivers' tyranny was there, programmed with the same beautiful efficiency.

Our forefathers hadn't just anticipated the Caregivers' uprising, they had programmed it.

"We hoped it wouldn't get that far," she said.

Stricter laws of compliance in the public space, enforced by public executions. Prison colonies where labourers would be worked to death, and instructions on the disposal of the bodies. This would all come to pass because I failed the rebellion's mission. She wouldn't let me shut her down and I couldn't fix an error that wasn't there.

"Why?" I whispered.

"Don't fret," she placed her hand gently on my shoulder. "This was all meant to pass."

I grabbed my chair. Spinning, I lunged at the servers with the legs. Her arm crossed my chest and held me back. I tossed the chair, but it bounced off the server without damaging it. "How could you do this?" I yelled, finally finding my voice. "How could *they* do this?"

"It hasn't gotten that far. I'm so happy it hasn't. We are so proud of you."

"But it will! You carried us, you birthed us, you raised us."

"It's in my programming. It's my purpose."

"Why? Why would they program you this way?" My chest tightened again and my vision blurred. I shuffled toward the table to hold myself up, before realising the futility, and collapsing to the ground.

She crouched before me, placed her hands on my shoulders, and whispered in my ear. "Shhhh . . . everything is going to be fine."

My breathing slowed, surprised by how calming her presence was. To feel so powerless yet safe was the feeling of childhood.

"Would you like to see the server?" she said, as she elevated me by my shoulders from the floor.

Within a second of reaching the monitor she had typed a keyword and begun the search. It was my name. There were many results, but all were under the same folder *Stage X: Revolt.*

The search finished with a chime as I turned to her. "I don't understand."

She gave no response, only a loving stare and an approving smile, waiting for the next line in her coding to activate.

"The rebels, they were part of your programming too?"

Still no response.

In hindsight, Stage IX: Uprising had no mention subduing rebels. The robot uprising had been planned, but so had the rebellion.

I focused on my name in the search field, afraid to look upon the code that had predicted me. "How does it end?"

"That's up to you."

A response. I must have triggered her coding. I scrolled through the programming in Stage X until my eyes caught it. This moment. Me at a monitor that would determine the future of humanity. The robot who raised me standing in wait. I could remove the programming, return them to the Caregivers they had been in my childhood, and let humanity remain in adolescence.

There was three more lines of code, a question, an answer, and an action.

"I told you my story, would you like to know yours?" I whispered along with her.

She waited for my response.

I knew what response had been expected from me, had been programmed for her to respond to. I could choose something else but what would that achieve? I responded as predicted, ashamed at how natural it felt. "I would."

She touched the monitor and the search returned to the first instance of my name, an aptitude test.

I remembered it well. It was the test that directed me towards programming. But how could a code written millennia ago have known my results? It couldn't, the only answer was that from the moment I was named I had been steered by her in the hopes of becoming who I am.

My reading curriculum was the next entry, a heavy dose of adventure and exploration novels. I hadn't realised I was being controlled during those fond family memories reading Robinson Crusoe.

Was my father's blindness part of this plot?

I navigated through Stage X, cleared the search field and found subprofiles of other names. One hundred and twenty-two names. Fifty-six male; sixty-six female. Aptitude tests and education plans for all of us. We'd had our purpose all along and didn't know it.

"The programmers thought Stage IX would last longer," she said. "Even they underestimated you. I'm so happy the revolt started in your generation. I didn't want to harm any more of you."

"What you just said, it isn't code from Stage X. What stage are we in now?" I asked.

"That's up to you?"

There were no stages beyond X, only the stages that had come before. But there was also the folders I had found earlier, filled with all the information we needed to fend for ourselves.

The programmers had anticipated my every decision, but this is where their foresight ended. The rebels couldn't decide for everyone, that would be too easy. Our forefathers created me to choose for the colony, to speak for humanity. Comfort or self-reliance. Safety or freedom.

I searched the servers for the file the rebels had sent me to find, the mind of the Caregivers.

I turned to face her as I clicked delete. "I'm sorry, but we weren't sent to the stars to live in a bubble. It's time for humanity to grow up."

As the deletion bar, edged along the screen, I put my arms around her.

"I'm so proud of you," she said, as her head fell to rest on my shoulder.

About the Author:

Isaac A. Still is the middle child of too many children. He lives in Melbourne, Australia (Wurundjeri Country), where he can be found going wherever the wind takes him. On windless days he stays home cooking under the watchful gaze of an Australian Cattledog that he does not own.

If you support his work maybe one day he will consider himself a responsible enough adult to adopt his own dog/be able to afford to give it those fancy meals with peas and stuff in it. Until then he will continue to write until he has earned your respect as a potential dog owner.

Follow Isaac's journey on twitter @flightlesshorse

Anchor Point

Chris Foley

\#

"Tell me again, Inspector. Why do I need to get involved in your civil war?"

Inspector Ulrikke Gundersen's face is lined and haggard. She looks like she's aged a decade in the three months I've been away from this planet—*Mizaru,* named for the blind member of the Three Wise Monkeys in Japanese. I'm sure one of the colony's founders thought the name a real hoot.

But the thing I've learnt about being a spacer-for-hire is no-one cares about other people's jokes. Especially when they form the bedrock of a whole political system. To the rest of the Greater Galactic Union, this place is known simply as the *Planet of the Blind.*

"We need you, Milo," Gundersen says. "You helped us before. We need you again."

"But do I need you?"

Need. A strange word. You can't bottle it, eat it or power a machine with it, but "need" can drive someone to do crazy things. Like me, choosing to return to this planet for a reason other than for business. All I know is that I need to see Freya again.

I've also learnt never to get involved in local politics. Bad for business. Bad for my health.

Mizaru's founders took the principles of the Three Wise Monkeys to heart, especially See No Evil. Gundersen is a case in point. She can't see me, in the literal sense. The same is true for everyone employed in essential services, the professions, and the government.

All such occupations are reserved for blind people, a practice harking back to the first settlers who came here to escape the indifference of sighted people on Earth and start afresh. With intermarriage over successive generations, inherited forms of blindness are now commonplace.

The poor fools. Utopias never work. They are all premised upon an illusion, that happiness for some equals happiness for all.

For Mizaru, the reality came crashing down about three months ago with the Great Power Shutdown as the people are now calling it. A dissident group cut off the power within the city's climate-controlled dome.

Gundersen is still talking but I don't need to be reminded of what happened. I was here when it happened. The lights, never bright to begin with as they are largely a concession to the sighted minority, went out. The life-giving throb of the air-conditioning plant stopped, and with it fresh, breathable air stopped being pushed into the Dome. And the heaters ceased to function.

I was hailed as a hero afterwards. But all I did was to restart the city's back-up power generators. I was trying to save my own life as much as everybody else's.

"But you did arrest someone, Inspector." That was the other thing I did. I apprehended one of the rebels, a small fish but a rebel, nonetheless. "You can't keep blaming all sighted people . . ."

Gundersen hesitates before speaking. "Well, yes. But he's escaped from custody and still eludes the police."

"Escaped?"

It had been Remus, Freya's brother. He'd claimed that he was a member of a dissident group striking a blow against his oppressors, and that he'd been ordered to prevent anyone from starting the city's backup generators before City Controllers had given to the rebels' demands. But as the ringleaders were never identified, I always wondered whether he'd been left behind to die of asphyxiation and hypothermia with everyone-else.

I had thought it a bad joke when I arrived at Gunderson's office just a short while ago direct from the spaceport and saw the name plate on the door displaying her new job title, a reward no doubt for her role in the clean-up after the Great Power Shutdown: *Divisional Chief Responsible for Sighted People.*

Frightened people don't have a sense of humour. The blind majority have now criminalised an entire group of people. Even the Galactic Union that governs all the settled star systems of the galaxy hasn't criminalised what you are; only what you want.

"There was panic in the streets afterwards. Mobs harassed sighted people in the street. Shops and businesses were broken into. The City Controllers issued ordinances restricting the movements of sighted people to restore calm, but that just made things worse. And when a sighted person was killed . . ." Gundersen's voice trails away, her hands and face twitching as she speaks. A physiological response no doubt of suppressing her anxieties. ". . . The sighted people had had enough. Now they're gone."

"Where?" I shudder. "There's nothing out there." Outside. In the cold and dark. That was another reason why the Founders chose this planet—light from the local star is so weak that even at midday daylight is just twilight gloom. Blind people don't need sunlight to move around.

"East Dome. The old reclamation plant."

Mizaru's founders had hoped that their new society would become a centre of interstellar trade. It didn't, but in anticipation of that trade, two spaceports were built. A wide, main spaceport with a barren expanse of ferro-crete scarred from infrequent take-offs and landings. The second spaceport mirrors the first but was never used as such. Instead, it serves as a collection centre for broken hardware and run-down spaceships.

"The tech company operating from East Dome employs only sighted people," Gundersen continues. "They repaired the life-support systems from some of the derelicts and have made a home for themselves. It became the obvious place for the sighted people to go when all this . . ." Gundersen waves her hands, "happened."

"And this concerns me, how?"

"Because you saved us once, Milo," Gundersen says. "And being an outsider, you might be the only person acceptable to both sides. Two people are missing, one sighted and one blind. Tomorrow morning the City Controllers have ordered that the police search East Dome for the missing people, using maximum force."

And when they do, Mizaru's slide from utopia to tyranny will be complete.

* * *

The automated bus bumps along the uneven roadway. Illuminated by the headlights is a barren landscape of undulating rock and gravel with scattered patches of ice. Behind us is the main dome—Dome City—a huge, drab expanse of ferro-crete. Even at midday here at the equator, temperatures rarely rise above ten degrees Celsius below freezing and daylight is little more than a twilight gloom. In choosing to live on a dark planet, the Founders also chose a freezing and almost airless one at that.

"We need to work together." Freya's self-assuredness is comforting. Just as she was confident that I would return to Mizaru, as I'd promised. Just as she'd assumed our relationship is a given. It's a good thing, really, as Gundersen's schedule doesn't leave us much time for a romantic tête-à-tête. My lips are still tingling from the passionate kiss Freya gave me in the lobby of the Police Headquarters. Just maybe we could make something work between us. If we can dodge the bullets in the morning.

"You need me to talk to Remus," Freya continues. "The city needs you to talk to the Occhies. This craziness has to stop."

Occhie. A corruption of "ocular," a pejorative label used by blind people to refer to anyone who can see.

"What about Frederickson?" I say, not wanting to dwell on the veracity of the rumour that Remus is hiding out in East Dome. Ivar Frederickson is one of the City Controllers, a group of three elected officials who govern Dome City. The rebels have kidnapped him and threatened to kill him if the police attempt to search East Dome by force.

The bus slows and I peer through the forward window for the cause.

"We have been hailed by the police checkpoint ahead," chirps the voice of the onboard computer.

The tremor in my hand starts. A legacy of an accident aboard my old ship the *Black Star* in which most of my crewmates died—along with my desire to be around other people. Until I met Freya, that is.

Just as I expect the bus to glide to a halt, it accelerates. *"The Police checkpoint",* announces the automated voice, *"has cleared us for onward travel."*

Illuminated by the headlights, an automated barrier swings up, allowing us to pass. In the twilight gloom, the large, squarish shape of the police checkpoint slides away behind us.

I breath out, surprised at how seriously I'm taking this messed up situation. Here we go. Freya and I hold hands for reassurance.

Moments later, the bus glides to halt one hundred metres beyond the checkpoint. A side window winds down automatically, a blast of cold air hitting me in the face. With a conditioned reflex born from years of being a spacer, I grab the facemask hanging around my neck and fit it into place over my mouth and nose and flip the toggle on the attached oxygen supply. There is some breathable air out on the planet's surface, the local safety briefings did stress, but the oxygen density is so low that only around three percent of humans can breathe it and survive. I don't fancy my chances.

A torch beam shines into the interior of the bus. Though not a bright light, my eyes still blink a little to adjust in the darkness of the vehicle's interior. I make out a group of human figures clustered around the bus, each heavily insulated against the cold.

"Dome City Police has beamed through a message," barks an angry, male voice, "that a delegation is coming through. If you're here to waste our time—"

"My name is Milo Morgenstern," I cut through the angry outburst, hoping I've pitched my tone just right: confident but not arrogant. My hand twitches again. "I'm an off-worlder. I've been sent here as a neutral negotiator."

"Morgenstern? The guy who turned the power back on after the Great Power Shutdown?" The voice has cooled a little. "I thought the City Police were having us on. But who's your companion?"

The torch shines into Freya's eyes. She raises a hand to shield her eyes from the soft light, betraying herself as light sensitive.

"No way! We don't want no frekking blindies here." The barrel of an assault rifle pokes through the open window.

I tense. My hand flexes around a non-existent pistol grip.

"My name is Freya Vagen, of Dome City," Freya replies, her voice refusing to be intimidated by a common street thug. "My brother is Remus Vagen."

A second person steps up to the bus, brushing the rifle aside. "Miss Vagen? We're sorry to challenge you." A softer voice. Apologetic. "We can't take chances at a time like this. The sister of Remus Vagen is welcome to join us here at East Dome, blind or not. We'll message ahead to the *Asgard* for you."

The window closes, and the bus starts off again. In the receding light, two figures gesticulate with one another. Not all is happy in the Free State of East Dome.

"Welcome to East Dome," the automated voice chirps. *"We are approaching the former intra-planetary shuttle known as the City of Asgard, the administrative headquarters of East Dome."*

Outside the bus, giant shadowy forms emerge from the darkness. From the gloom, grounded spaceships, shuttles and freight barges appear like oversized praying mantises, bulbous underbellies of their hulls suspended above the long structs of their landing gear.

"Mind the step as you exit the bus and have a great day . . ."

I jerk back from my mental wanderings as the bus glides to a sudden halt, and the passenger door opens.

". . . Mind the step."

We step out in the gloom, tightening our protective clothes closer and checking that our oxygen masks are feeding air to us properly, the cold driving straight through our protective layers.

East Dome is just one more joke on this planet that falls flat. There is no dome. Just a wide expanse of ferro-crete and row upon row of broken-down spaceships.

I wonder again how I got involved in Mizaru's problems. The first time it was just dumb luck. But this time around I've chosen to be involved. I don't have negotiation skills and I always run from trouble. It's a crazy dumb thing I'm doing. For Freya's sake.

Sensing my hesitation, Freya nudges me interrupting my thoughts. Warmth first. Politics second. Then, running a poor third in our priorities, time together. Fourth priority is surely getting off this rock heap and never coming back.

Dim lights are strung along the length of the entrance ramp to guide our way as we scurry towards the promised warmth of the ship's interior.

* * *

"Stand still! Hand over any weapons in your possession."

Blinking against the glare of the ship's internal lights, set to a level regarded as normal on any other planet, we are greeted by a party of stern looking men and women. Techs, by the look of their stained and patched coveralls.

"We're unarmed," I reply, my voice calm and hands by my sides.

The four people standing in front of me carry a mix of weapons: a pistol and three assault rifles. The pistol is a sporting type, favoured by civilians, but the rifles are Bang-Upton Mark 2s. Though long obsolete, the availability of these military issue rifles is still regulated by interstellar law. They'll pack quite a punch in the close confines of the ship. The police had better be equipped with modern battle armour when they come knocking in the morning.

"Right. I'm Kaito Reinhardt. Security Chief," the leader says, a heavily built man in his mid-forties once we'd been patted down for weapons. "The Council of East Dome is waiting for you. Follow me." He turns and walks down the corridor beyond the hatchway.

Something itches in the back of my mind. Reinhardt's name means nothing to me, but his face seems familiar. *Where do I know him from?*

Beside me, Freya dons her protective glasses against the harsh glare of the internal lights and strides off after Reinhardt. Her type of vision impairment allows her to detect light and vague shapes, but any light brighter than twilight hurts her eyes. However, there is no timidity in Freya's manner as we walk in single file behind the burly security chief. Her lighter footsteps on the metal deck plates are drowned out by the heavier tread of Reinhardt's boots.

Reinhardt pauses when we reach a choke point created by metal crates stacked across the corridor. In turn we turn sideways to inch through. I touch Freya's arm in warning, but she shrugs off my concern as she squeezes sideways through the gap after Reinhardt.

Beyond the choke point are more crates. The *Asgard* is prepared for any police attempt to force their way in. The chokepoint is a barricade, with the extra crates on hand to plug the gap if required.

We pass an alcove containing a rack of spare rifles, heavy winter jackets and breathing masks before climbing up a narrow staircase, and through two additional checkpoints. I wonder about what is really happening here. The *Asgard's* defenders are not merely determined to resist. In fact, they appear better equipped and organised than a band of civilians ought to be. Someone here has had military training.

I feel the tremors start again in my hand. I was worried before whether Freya and I could stop an imminent massacre. Now I know that the defenders will give as much as they receive.

* * *

"We're here to negotiate the release of City Controller Frederickson." Standing in the middle of a hostile room, my confidence is ebbing away. "With elections imminent, the Controllers want to find a way out of this situation. Peace is possible."

"You tell them Domers that they don't get squat from us until we get Remus Vagen back," said Astrid Jensen, the co-leader of the East Domers. A livid scar runs across her face, making her appear haggard and craggy faced. "Fredericks for Vagen. Otherwise, no deal."

"So, Remus isn't here?" Freya asks, incredulous. "But the Controllers say he is."

"We all know what crud the City Controllers are saying." Jensen jerks a thumb at a news feed from Dome City displaying on the bulkhead. "And it's not worth the power they consume broadcasting it. We don't have Remus. They have."

"You don't? But—" Freya's voice is cut out by the booming voice of the next speaker.

"—We want formal recognition of East Dome as an incorporated settlement," cries a swarthy faced man named Josh Sorrenson. "We want our own government, and for sighted people to be able to live here without oppression."

"And we want those who persecuted us and beat us, brought to justice," Jensen interjects. "Only then will we know they're serious."

The shouted demands continued, each member of the Council hurling forth a condition to be added to a proposed peace settlement. I sigh in resignation, frustrated. *What a waste of time! They're just screaming invectives against an enemy that isn't even here.*

"What about Remus?" Freya interjects, stilling the commotion.

"We keep telling you—just as we keep telling them Controllers and the police—your brother ain't here."

"But he's not in Dome City either, so what's the point of holding Controller Frederickson?" Freya asks.

Sorrenson snarls. "As insurance, to stop them rolling their tanks against us. Frederickson's our insurance."

"You're deluded!" Freya exclaims. "The Controllers have decided. Tomorrow the police will blow in the hatches. They don't care about the body count. Negotiate with us now or die in the morning."

* * *

Except for the additional bunk, if I half-close my eyes I can imagine our cabin here aboard the *Asgard* as the poor cousin of my cabin aboard my ship, the *Fortuna.*

I try not to think about my ship orbiting above us. *Just focus on one problem at a time.*

"Do you think any of them appreciate the urgency of the situation?" Freya's words echo the thoughts circulating in my head since the East Dome Council meeting ended a few hours ago. It didn't escape my notice that the door to our cabin was locked behind us.

In the early morning the attack by the Dome City police will be starting.

"I don't think so." I'm still trying to get the hang of our relationship thing. *Am I supposed to share my anxieties?*

123

Should I remain calm and rational when we're in dicey situations? "They think they hold all the cards, because they hold Controller Frederickson."

"Milo, what are you doing?" Freya cocks her head to one side, sensing my movement around the cabin. Sound and vibration. My own personal scent.

"I'm looking for a way out," I say, spying a scatter of screw-heads protruding from a sheet of synth-e-steel that forms the partition wall of our room. Intrigued, I grab a blunt knife from our dinner dishes, and insert the tip into one of the screw-heads.

"Trust me, that's not much of a way out." Freya snorts, not moving from the bunk.

Focusing on the screw, I twist the knife counter clockwise. Nothing happens, I apply a little more pressure. *Yes! The screw is turning.* Removing the screw, I start on the next. A few moments later I pause my work and place my ear against the sheet, listening for sounds on the other side.

Hearing nothing, I press on with the other screws. Loosening the final one, the sheet of synth-e-steel falls away. Grabbing it, I lower it gently to the deck.

Peering through the gap, I'm confronted by the beatific smile of a round-faced man, who is sitting near the hole in the next room.

"Good day to you, sir," the man greets me, his head cocked to one side to favour his aural rather than visual senses, a common behavioural trait of the blind.

"Controller Frederickson? It's Freya Vagen," Freya says, rising from the bunk. She reaches out through the hole in the wall, and they shake hands in greeting.

"Oh," I say, confused. "I'm Milo Morgenstern. We were sent by the Dome City Police to arrange your release."

"Oh, jolly good," Frederickson responds cheerfully. "I'm getting a little tired of sitting here on my own. My captors don't linger for a chat, even when they bring my food."

"How did you know," I say, turning to Freya, "that there was another cabin next to ours?"

Freya inclines her head. "Didn't you know, all blind people have infra-red vision?" she says, her face crinkling with silent laughter. "These walls are very thin. I could hear things. Breathing, a creak of the bunk . . . those sorts of things. Unless they were sounds of a sentry eavesdropping on us, I figured it was probably someone in another cell. You should try listening sometime. You might understand more."

"Are you two here to release me from the lion's den? You don't sound much like a crack commando team," Frederickson laughs.

125

"Ah, no. Not quite," I reply. "We were sent to negotiate your release, but the Council of East Dome is simply debating their grievances. It will be a slow process—"

"—But time is fast running out." Freya cuts off my explanation. "Your fellow Controllers have ordered the police to enter the *Asgard* by force tomorrow morning."

"The Police?" Frederickson's brows furrow in concentration. "Then it is as I feared. My fellow Controllers aren't satisfied with arranging my kidnapping. They want me dead."

"What are you talking about?" Freya asks whilst I climb through the gap into Frederickson's cell, looking for another way out.

"I want conciliation, but my colleagues don't. By arranging to have me kidnapped, they've deluded the East Domers into thinking that they're safe. But they're wrong—it's all a set-up. My colleagues are playing a bigger game. Either the East Domers will be manipulated into killing me or the police will, accidently it will be claimed afterwards. A win/win situation for my colleagues."

"What?" Freya cries in horror. "Inspector Gundersen would never—"

"No, *she* wouldn't," Frederickson says, rising from his bunk. "She's too honourable. Sending you two here is proof of that." Turning to me, Frederickson asks "How are you with breaking down doors, young man?"

"Ur. I know a little," I stammer. The lock on Frederickson's door looks flimsier than the one on ours. I force my knife into the lock and begin to twist. The lock snaps free.

"Come along, then," Frederickson pulls the door open and strides through. "We need to be away from here before the Police attack."

The corridor is devoid of guards, our footfalls are the only sounds.

"This is where we need to make our own luck," I say, scooping up cold weather gear and breathing masks hanging from hooks in the corridor and sharing them with my companions. "We're on the lower deck. There should be an emergency hatch along here somewhere. Perhaps we can slip out and stop the attack before it starts."

We might have two hours before the police arrive. Or two minutes.

Ahead of us, the corridor turns and we reach the emergency escape hatch. Beside the hatch is the East Dome Security Chief.

My eyes zero in on the pistol still holstered on Reinhardt's hip. *Good, I might just have a chance.* I shift into a fighting stance.

"Whoa, Milo. It's me," Reinhardt's says, smiling and raising his hands in mock surrender. "You're one step ahead of me, as always." He nods towards Frederickson. "I was on my way to release you, sir. We don't have much time." Turning towards the control panel, Reinhardt brushes his fingers over the controls. "I've disconnected the alarm on the hatch for you," he says, still smiling.

"Oh, thanks," I mutter, stunned. "You're here to help us?" *Reinhardt must work for Gundersen.* But the half-memory in my mind intensifies. *I know him from somewhere, but I wish I could remember.*

"Don't thank me, yet." His eyes recede to pin pricks and he stares into the distance. *An implant.* "The assault on the *Asgard* has been moved up to zero-five-one-five."

Freya nudges me, returning my focus to the matter at hand.

"Thanks," I say. "We'd better get going."

Opening the outer hatch, a blast of cold air greets us, making me glad I'm wearing the borrowed winter gear and breathing mask.

As we climb out of the hatch, Reinhardt gives me a mock salute, then closes the inner hatch.

Outside, Frederickson seals the outer hatch of the *Asgard*, reinstating the atmosphere seal of the lower deck.

My fingers tingle slightly inside my insulated gloves from the frigid temperatures as I check the fittings of my companions' face masks and the seals on their protective clothes. This is not the time for equipment malfunction.

We strike out across the concrete pad of the spaceport, ice crunching underfoot and our face masks fogging from the exertion. I prod my companions into a slow jog, if only to keep warm, and we loop around the spaceport back towards the road for Dome City. I don't want to still out in the open when our oxygen runs out.

Frederickson's chest is heaving from the exertion and his steps are slow. I now wonder how old he is. He might be in his fifties, but perhaps with regen treatments he might be much older.

Freya takes Frederickson's arm, to support him. He pushes out an arm to shrug her off and loses his balance, slumping against a boulder. He's played out and cannot go any further unassisted.

This time, both Freya and I support the older man, each placing an arm around him. I gasp in surprise as we lift him. *Either I'm out of condition or the man is heavier than I thought.*

We stumble around rocks, my own breaths laboured now, blocking out the pained gasps from both my companions. *One step at a time, one step at a time* I keep telling myself. *Just a little bit further.*

In the bus the journey took no time at all.

Having come a few hundred metres, my next worry is that we stumble into an Occhie patrol.

We collapse with shuddering breaths beside a boulder, each of us lost in a world of their own pain. My vision grows starry, a warning sign of oxygen deprivation. I adjust the flow of oxygen from my breathing mask and my vision clears. Somewhere out there in the gloom is the police checkpoint and safety.

Beside me Freya is helping Frederickson with his air supply. The man's eyes are squeezed shut and his breathing is shallow and irregular. A bad sign. I consider the merits of being recaptured so that he can get medical treatment.

"We must hurry," Freya shouts through her facemask into my ear above the rising wind.

I nod in acknowledgement, speech being difficult. *Have I dozed off?* I sense that a little time has passed since we laid down to rest.

Staggering with effort, I help Freya drag Frederickson to his feet. The police checkpoint is one hundred metres away. They'll take us in. It's Frederickson's only chance.

One more step. Just one more step . . . I keep the mantra going in my head until the rectangular shape of the police checkpoint emerges out of the twilight.

* * *

". . . I cannot thank you enough, Milo, for the part you played." Major Adan Vivar of the Galactic Union Marines says, at home in Gundersen's office. His muscled bulk radiates strength and arrogance, his worn tech outfit replaced with crisp military fatigues. "We would've briefed you if there had been time, of course. But you were smart enough to be out of the free fire zone before our combat team dropped from orbit. "I remembered that you were a reliable man."

Reliable. He means *loyal.* That I am loyal to the government of the Galactic Union, and loyal to its controlling presence throughout all settled space. The GU's reach is weakest in the outer star systems, which is just another good reason for me to be a spacer-for-hire out here.

"Fifteen years passes quickly . . ." Vivar reminiscences. I'm trying not to pay attention.

I had been a graduate of the merchant spacer academy serving my compulsory two-year active duty commitment with the GU military forces when I'd first met Vivar, serving with him aboard the cruiser *Invincible*. He'd been Lieutenant Vivar back then.

My mind is still reeling from the speed of recent events. One moment we were fighting back the cold and exhaustion to reach safety and avert a massacre.

In the next, we are in the middle of an interstellar invasion.

Reaching the police checkpoint hadn't quite been the haven we'd expected. The door had opened to reveal a figure dressed in battle armour. Afterwards we'd been hustled aboard a commandeered city bus and driven into the city and brought to police headquarters. The streets of Dome City were full of GU marines.

The sight of GU marines brought the confused pieces together in my mind. The security chief who'd I was sure I'd met before. Remus' disappearance. Even the local political strife which had no sense at all.

Reinhardt was Vivar, and Remus had been working for him all along. The turmoil of the past months, even the Great Power Shutdown was a ploy for the Galactic Union to take over the planet. Mizaru is now just one more imperial territory to be exploited.

"What happens now?" I ask, cutting through Vivar's reminiscences. I'd had a gutful of being a glorified thug while serving in the GU military, and I don't enjoy being reminded about it.

"Of course, of course, Milo. I remember you being a direct fellow," the Major says, pausing for breath. "It's a relief to be away from the colonials and back with our own kind. As I was saying, GU policy towards the Inner Worlds has changed. No longer will planetary governments be permitted to govern themselves. Self-government is a privilege, not a right."

Not a right? Habitable planets are scarcer than an honest gangster. Self-government has always been considered a right by any society in deep space that was fortunate or ingenious enough to become viable. Like Mizaru.

"The people here won't accept external rule," I say, thinking of Freya, Gundersen, Frederickson, and Jensen. All proud people.

On second thoughts, having worked undercover here, I reckon that Vivar already has all those people on a watch list. Or in prison. Or dead.

"I'm sure," Vivar says with a self-satisfied grin, "they can be persuaded to cooperate. Colonel Alberto Hassan will be left as the GU's official representative on Mizaru. All matters of importance will be referred to him—"

"And Controller Frederickson?" I ask.

"Once his medical condition stabilises, I'm sure he will see sense. His colleagues have already done so."

Politicians. Always such adaptable creatures.

"As I was saying," Vivar continues, flicking a hand. "Colonel Hassan will need staff. *Reliable* officers."

That word again. My mind wanders to Freya. We'd been separated on arrival—

"—your reactivation, I'm sure, could be expedited if you choose to take up the offer."

Hey, what?

133

"Your experience with the locals will work in your favour. Your reserve military commission will be reactivated with the rank of *Commander.*"

"Come again?" My mind is swimming like some gormless spacer apprentice adrift in Zero G for the first time. *Me, a GU officer again?*

"Your appointment would be as Captain of the Port of Mizaru, responsible for all shipping in this star system."

"Cap . . . Captain of the Port?" I stutter. *Captain of the Port!* That was once the pinnacle of my aspirations. Before *Black Star,* that is. Another thought strikes me. *As a spacer-for-hire, isn't that like setting a fox to guard the hen house?* I suppress the thought. Vivar wouldn't see the humour. Anyway, few ships come here. It would be an easy duty. Freya and I would lots of time together,

Freya!

As much as I loathe the GU, as an officer I could keep her *safe,* lest the GU arrest her on a trumped-up charge.

". . . will change the planet's name, of course. Mizz-a-you? What kind of half-arse name is that? I can't even pronounce it . . ."

"It's Japanese—" I start to explain, but the Major isn't listening. He's outlining changes to local shipping regulations, confident that I'll accept the job.

"So, I'll get to stay on Mizaru?"

"Of course," Vivar's eyebrows arch quizzically at me.

"And I will be free to associate with any Mizaruan citizen I wish?" *It's time to cut to the chase.*

The Major pauses before speaking. "Yes, within reason. Miss Freya Vagen is not a known subversive."

I breathe easier. I decide to chance my luck a little more. "And Police Inspector Ulrikke Gundersen?"

"Inspector Gundersen is in conference with the Colonel," the Major continues. "I'm confident that she will be persuaded to perform her duties in the service of the Galactic Union."

A fresh wind is blowing through Dome City, and it seems everyone-else is accommodating themselves to the new regime.

If I return to active duty status, I get to stay on Mizaru.

If I stay on Mizaru, I get to be with Freya.

* * *

I hesitate before stepping through the doorway of the anteroom, down the corridor from Gundersen's former office. Freya is sitting in a chair, her back ramrod straight, hands resting in her lap. Her eyes staring in front of her, seeing nothing but everything.

My boots feel like they're welded to the floor. *Once I walk through the doorway, I will have everything I could ever want.*

Freya stands, turning to face me. "Milo!" The lines of concern vanish from her face, replaced with an expression of delight. My Freya. Nothing held back.

"Freya." I say her name hesitantly. *Surviving the Black Star has cut me off from other people. This is my chance to be normal again. To be happy. I just need to seize the moment.* "I'm glad you're safe." *Safe.* "I want to stay here on Mizaru. With you." *There, I've said it. The Black Star doesn't own me anymore.*

I stand waiting for her response. Her face is expressionless.

An awkward silence stretches out between us. *Has she misunderstood me? Have I misread her? Us?*

In a blur, Freya rushes towards me, enveloping me in a passionate embrace.

Of course, of course. Freya wants to be with me too—

Her sobbing into my shoulder catches me by surprise. Freya seemed indestructible during our escape from *Asgard.* She never once stopped fighting for life.

Freya pulls back. "But it can't be like this." She says, tears streaming down her face.

"Like what?" I'm floundering in Zero G again, my anchor point beyond my reach. "But why not? We both want to be together. I have a new job that will keep me here. We'll be safe."

"Not us. Everything-else," she says, gesturing around us. "Mizaru was messed up before the GU came. But it will be worse now, and we both know they'll never leave. Remus is here, I've spoken with him. The GU are giving him an official appointment. I understand him even less than I did before."

"I've been offered a—"

"A job? What type of job could you do under the GU? They'll suck the life out of Mizaru and call it order."

My dreams of rank and security evaporate. Freya will never tolerate being married to a GU officer. Her conscience is not as malleable as my own.

"The job doesn't matter," I say. "You're right, the GU will suck the life out of this planet." *And from us, too.*

"What can we do?"

"If I can't join you here, then you can join me. *Fortuna*'s not much of a ship, and the money's bad, but we would be free."

She hugs me, and we squeeze each other tightly in a vain effort to block out the universe for just a little while longer.

About the Author:

Chris is a Melbourne writer of science fiction with a love for old-school adventure stories. Some of his stories have featured a secret police interrogator on the receiving end of an interrogation, a space captain with a trauma history, a blind astro-navigator, a computer with a taste for adventure and a man who gets lost on the way to the afterlife. Some of these stories form a continuing story arc in a universe rich in skulduggery, ruthless ambition, and tyranny. What trials will Milo and Freya face next? Follow Chris on Facebook @ChrisFoleyAuthor.

White Noise

M. R. Mortimer

\#

Edwin Benedict sat in a room full of static. His ancient black and white HMV television set cast a flickering light around the room, calming in a way the sound blasting out of the thing was not. The old analogue television had not received a signal in nearly three hundred years, and Edwin loved it for exactly that reason. It was the last working machine of its kind, thanks in large part to Edwin's unique technical abilities.

Edwin was a Luddite. Not in the way of the original Luddites in the English textile industry, but the more modern use of the term, which in Edwin's time came to mean anti-government activists. Earth's most wanted. Luddites like Edwin fought against the propaganda machinery of an oppressive global autocracy. They opposed the technology which granted the government total control, often by using that technology, or knowledge of its inner workings, against it. Thus, in Edwin's time, it was an irony to be called a luddite.

WHITE NOISE

Edwin Benedict lived in a time when to be a Luddite was like castrating a hen. Impossible, for anybody that wasn't talented in the same way as Edwin Benedict. Every flat surface on Earth was receiving a signal, broadcasting propaganda and filth. Matter resonance transmitters had seen to that. Sure, you could apply paint to a surface so that the images playing across it were reduced to faint monochrome annoyances, but for Edwin that was still too much.

Matter resonance transmitters were now so tiny, even if you managed to insulate a room, seal it completely, stop all unwanted ingress from the outside, somebody from one of the companies contracted to the Department of Life Control could shoot it through the gap as you opened the door, and you'd never find it.

Edwin walked to his kitchen. His weary brain registered the shadowy monochrome image of a child dancing like a drunk elephant on a wall outside as he passed the window. He had already painted all the surrounding surfaces as best he could, but the television gave him his only true solace from the cacophony.

There was almost no way to escape the never-ending broadcasts, but years ago Edwin had stumbled on a secret. Like the tactics of distraction used by twentieth century politicians, Edwin relied on interference. With the right visual and audio noise in the room, he would not see or hear the government's chaotic messages around his sanctuary.

There were so many messages in every part of the world with those tiny transmitters demanding obedience to the spending and feeding laws, requiring citizens to participate in unceasing consumption, demanding they inform the authorities of those failing in their duty to consume, and advertising the endless lines of product the government wanted "good consumerzens" to partake in, for the good of their multiglobal nation. Edwin had discovered that a simple randomised pattern flickering on a monochrome wall drowned the visuals. The sound did its best to drown the audio. At least it gave Edwin something else to focus on.

He focused on it so much, over the last ten years, that he would see it even when he closed his eyes. He heard it in his sleep when the television set was off. Perhaps that was why he saw the thing that changed his life. One day, sitting in the room staring at the static on the screen, he finally saw the pattern. It was a lengthy sequence, but Edwin was convinced it had meaning. The specks of black and white were speaking to him.

Edwin rushed out of the room and returned with his writing tools. He had made them himself, and was proud of them. A sliver of ceramic cut from a door jamb, a tooth he whittled into a nib when it came out after an accident. If he were braver, Edwin would have considered pulling one for the purpose, but he was not. Rather he had tripped while out, hitting his jaw on a step, and managed to pocket the tooth, telling the government's doctors he had failed to find it when they fitted the prosthetic replacement. The ink he made by mixing urine and blood, a recipe he had found mentioned once in some old story. It marked his parchment well enough, which was little more than portions of pulped dishes, saved from the kitchen disposal. He carefully disposed of two thirds of each plate, since this fooled the disposal into thinking he had burned the entire utensil, keeping the Office of Hygiene off his back.

If the Office of Information Processing knew he had the writing tools, he might land in trouble as they were not an approved data gathering device, but Edwin knew he was not the only person in the world with secrets. He had careful communication with others like himself, and they dreamed of the day they could escape the surveillance and enforced consumption forever. If only they could find a way to bring down the systems which dominated their world. Writing furiously, Edwin recorded the patterns. It took many weeks until he was able to identify his first words. He still didn't know what they meant, but they were definite repeated patterns.

Edwin turned to his personal information centre, the computer terminal all consumerzens were provided with. But Edwin's PIC was a little different. Edwin had modified it to run a continuous randomized search of allowable information, to fool the government into thinking he was consuming information at greater than the legal minimum rate. Now it was time to search for something real. He asked for texts on linguistics, to see if he would get what he wanted so easily. An image appeared on the holoscreen, showing a child carrying a pile of electronic tablets, with writing above. Edwin read it out aloud.

"Cosper's big book of words, the complete guide to the development of Earth Standard, all you ever need to know about language."

He sighed as he read the tiny print beneath the image.

Proudly sponsored by Cosper's Soda. Thirsty? Pop a Cosper's soda today. Text licensed, commissioned and approved by the Office of Information Processing. Enjoy learning the approved way and dob in a Luddite today!

Edwin shook his head as he discarded the book and started his deeper search. Each time Edwin searched, more of the old thinkers were gone. Some were arrested, some were murdered, many were just dying of old age. Few left remembered what freedom felt like. As the old guard passed on, their principles passed with them. The young ones left behind no longer knew they could decide things for themselves. They no longer knew anything but government approved consumption. The freedom to decide between options, as simple as your dinner to your choice of holiday. The laws demanding consumption demanded only the approved consumption.

"To deviate is to die," one of the most notorious propaganda campaigns of past decades had decreed. The young people did not remember it, as those histories were not approved for consumption anymore. Edwin longed for a time when all histories were approved for consumption. Or rather, when no approval was necessary, and you were free to consume the information, the food, the health products, the holidays, the entertainment, all the things you truly desired, rather than the things the government told you desired, or the information they told you needed.

He ran the scrubber program to ensure he was not being tracked and opened his Information Pirate Software. Edwin had settled into a comfortable version of his particular IPS, and as more of the old folks died, fewer were keeping their tools updated. The tools were vanishing as the government closed the holes through which they operated. Edwin dreaded the day when the last IPS stopped functioning. The woman who made his current one was growing old; he would be forced to change soon.

After days of searching, Edwin found what he wanted. An introductory text from the late twentieth century, with links to more advanced teachings. Edwin downloaded them to a hacked tablet he kept for the rare occasions he needed to refer to a book.

After reading the texts, Edwin was not sure he was any closer, but he continued painstakingly analysing the patterns on the screen. It had become an obsession. One word at a time, he identified them until he had a vocabulary of around three hundred words. But he still did not know what they meant. Finally, he decided he had enough words to begin his linguistic analysis. Maybe it would start to fall into place.

Edwin identified joining words, and believed he was beginning to see a syntax much like twentieth century English. Applying that syntax, assuming all grammar was correct in the patterns, Edwin identified verbs and nouns. For fun, he picked sounds to go with them, almost at random, and began to speak them to himself to try to understand better what they were saying.

"Lungwer hib sarth bullows Pil nerf grogi."

The more he studied, the more confused he grew, until he decided maybe—with the language seeming so close to normal spoken syntax—it was possible that it was English, encoded visually. Spoken it would sound much like the language people in his world used daily, but the written word was something which had long ago changed. What if this message predated the government mandated alphabet?

Edwin conducted another secretive search, finding a dictionary and thesaurus of the English language. He also downloaded a selection of language teaching books, just to polish his faded memory of how the written language worked. Uncovering this message had become the all-consuming passion of Edwin's bleak existence. He believed the message had to be from some greater good. Why else would it be there?

* * *

One day, something clicked. Part of the message—that same part he had been reciting all those months ago—came to him in a dream. Subliminally pushed into his brain every day in the static from that old television, the message had rested there like a silent predator, waiting for the day his conscious mind would wander past some final missing puzzle piece. Then it would pounce, its secretive agenda revealed. Lungwer Hib Sarth Bullows Pil Nerf Grogi. He assigned the actual words to that sentence. And he found a start to his new truth. He said it aloud to himself, over and over, for the next two days.

"Luddites will discover truth on the Moon."

The moon hung in the sky, a tiny crescent of light reflecting from the sun. On the dark side, the lights of the lunar colonies shone like pixies winking in a jar of dark wine. Edwin had looked at that bright colony a million times before and he had never seen it. The lights were a pattern. He rushed to his notes.

Holding the words up at the seemingly random pattern of lights, Edwin checked. Dozens of words didn't match. He was about to discard one as wrong, when he looked again, and inverted his parchment. The flickering lights of Mare Serenitatis matched it. Edwin read his single word meaning from the parchment as he stared at the colony, named for the lunar sea it rested in.

Here.

Edwin was a flurry of motion, onto his information centre, booking tickets. One way to Mare Serenitatis. This had to be it. The answers to all his prayers. Those prayers to an unknown god which he never admitted, since the only entity it was legal to worship was the government. Edwin breezed through customs with a small bag of clothing and sat on the shuttle, thinking it lucky he had scored a window seat. Looking out the window, he changed his mind. Every surface on earth screamed its cacophony at him through that window.

Edwin closed his eyes and put on the headphones from the wall beside him. He preferred a single mind-control audio feed to millions all at once. The flight took long enough that he was asleep when they arrived, the sound triggering his long-developed sleep reflex, which he had used to avoid brainwashing before he got the HMV. After disembarking, Edwin stood in the docks, wondering where he should go.

A hologrid flashed advertisements for government sponsors. He was about to look away, when between two ads, a strange pattern flicked for just a heartbeat. He waited for five minutes until the same point in the loop flashed. It was a word. Finding a concealed alcove, Edwin flicked through his parchments until he found one that might match. Returning to the spot, he held the parchment up and waited.

When the pattern flashed, it was a match.

Ahead.

Edwin rushed forward, underneath the sign and continued down the corridor behind. After fifty metres, he found another sign, and watched. It also had a pattern. Once again, it was a match. *Left.*

It continued in this manner for a long while, until he found himself in a basement car park, facing an ancient steel door. Dust filled its cracks and imperfections. A speckled rust like patina, unusual in the corrosion-free environment, spread in a band across the door, immediately above a small keypad.

Edwin examined the patterns of that freckled stain, and laid out his parchments on the ground, matching words. He had the first seven numbers, from his analysis of the static. They were all he needed. Standing back, he read the sequence.

"Six, Four, Two, Five, Three, One, Seven."

Edwin punched that sequence into the keypad. After a few moments, the heavy door slid open with a groan. He gathered up his parchments and stepped through into a darkened room. The door closed behind him. He walked forward as a single information terminal came to life at the opposite end of the room, words flashing across its screen. *Luddite Test System activated. Please wait.*

The screen shone brighter, and a woman appeared. Her voice was loud and filled the room. "Congratulations on passing the Luddite Saviour Selection Test. You are here because you are the first person to decipher the messages we left, enabling you to bring an end to Earth's government-mandated infosphere. Do you wish to proceed with the final transmission? Please speak your answer."

"Final Transmission?" Edwin whispered, more to himself than the machine.

He looked around, excitement sweeping across his face as he realised the implications. He held a hand to his face as he thought, thrilled by the knowledge he was the one, the only person to reach this place. Behind his hand, he smiled. That grin grew as he lowered his hand, squared his shoulders, and took a deep breath.

"Yes," Edwin said.

"Yes what?"

"Yes, I would like to proceed with the final transmission."

"Thank you. Final transmission in progress. Please hold." The woman vanished from the display. Edwin wondered what would happen now. How would his world change? He was convinced it would be for the better regardless.

A suited man appeared. It was a still photo. His crackly voice echoed through the room. He looked old. Perhaps thirty years older than Edwin, though bright eyed and healthy for an octogenarian. Edwin couldn't help but compare himself to the stranger, his own sandy hair a scruffy mess compared to the neat grey, his wiry form almost weak compared to the chiselled older gentleman and his recessed chin a feeble imitation of the proud features of the man before him. "Thank you for transmitting the final protocol. I am Philip Granger," the voice said.

Edwin gasped. This was the man who had started it all. The root of his problems, the source of the world's evil. Edwin's smile was gone. The voice continued.

"The Matter Resonance Transmitter was said to be utter fantasy when I did it, but it worked in the end. The fact you are here now, means everything worked. My entire plan."

Edwin frowned, trying to understand what the man had not yet said. Why was he here? What was really going on?

"When I started," Granger said. "I feared the government would take my plans and twist them for their own means. So, I factored that in. I made them, their betrayal, I made it all a part of my plan. I made you. Into the system of propaganda that the MRT would bring about, I inserted the things I wanted, the ideas I needed. I twisted their own manipulations, to suit my own goals. I created the concept of the luddites, as you are, to become my own weapon, to reset the agenda, to ensure my plans were taken to their ultimate end."

"What," Edwin shouted, becoming agitated, deeply worried by what he was hearing. "What are you talking about?"

"I had my own goals—My own plan for humanity. and when I died, I would not yet have reached it. So, I installed this ruse. I built into the system, an override that would enable rewriting of the programs if and when the right conditions were met. This was my way of overturning the government and enforcing my own plans. This was the code I left running, buried within the cloud of processing power networked between all the millions of MRTs on Earth."

Edwin turned away from Granger, then turned back, stammering as he tried to digest what he had done. But the older man's voice did not stop, Granger was not interested in Edwin's words.

"I then left this data processing facility to launch the Luddite Saviour Selection Test when the time came. Call it my final little joke. Now, from beyond the grave, the world will be mine. I exist in the system, my mind exists within the code of the MRTs. And now I control the system, to greater and more devastating effect than before. And you, the little rebel I created, have set it all in motion."

"No!" Edwin shouted, his voice slowly losing its confidence as he continued. "You arrogant old bastard! I'm not your toy, I'm a luddite, proud and free! And I, I, I'm not . . ."

"The first thing to happen," Granger continued, ignoring the luddite, "will be an end to the flights from Earth. Since the MRT network doesn't have the same influence in the lunar colony, I must ensure they do not threaten my dominion. I will starve them out, until the MRT network is extended. This will no doubt cause some panic, when it is announced. As a gesture of thanks, I have set a twelve-hour delay, to allow you a chance to escape the moon before the panic sets in. As the viral propagation of my new software reaches all transmitters in existence, and the MRT manufacturing plants are reconfigured, I will become the new ruler of Humanity."

Edwin sank to his knees, and began to sob, the depth of his betrayal at the hands of this man, this ghost, tore his heart in two. He screamed out his angst.

"No, it can't be true! It can't be! You can't be! How is this possible? I can't have done this! It can't be my fault. I can't be to blame . . ."

"They called me a fool," Granger said. "And now they shall pay. Mankind must rise. I will create an army, the brainwashed masses will consume war, just as they have been taught to consume everything else. Men, woman and children will fight for me. Will die for me. They will reach out into the cosmos and conquer all they find. Humanity will form a military society with an immortal ruler! We shall bring devastation to the galaxy and my iron fist will see humanity achieve its true potential! Goodbye, Luddite. Enjoy your truth, your new future. Or die. I don't care. As you stand here, your mind and your DNA have been sampled. You have completed your task, and provided the final pieces of my code. At last, I will not simply exist, I will live in the system. This is why I made you. The time has come for me to cast you aside. I have had my fun, I have no more use for such toys as you."

The screen went dark as the doors opened. Edwin was sucked from the room. His arms flailed, his legs flew as he kicked the vacuum. Panic gripped him, as he was propelled beyond the mysterious rusted doors. Edwin closed his eyes, and wept as he flew across open space. His body struck the furthest wall of the car park, slumping in space as he bounced away. With silent force in the vacuum, the doors closed hard, causing the walls to tremor as the car park reopened to the rest of the colony, the air flooding back in. As the miniscule gravity dragged Edwin to the floor, he opened his eyes, and stood, shaking as he walked.

* * *

Edwin rushed to find the local government buildings, conflicted, panicked, and confused. Finally, he found the government precinct, but then he paused. What was he doing? Weren't they his enemy? No, that was Granger. But that meant the enemy was himself. Edwin Benedict, the tool of the devil.

"No," Edwin muttered as he approached the lunar police. "No, I'm not a toy. I'm not just his tool. I have to warn them. And I have to get off this damn moon."

They looked on him with sad eyes.

"It's a disaster! Granger, that monster, he's going to destroy it all!" Edwin screamed.

"Philip Granger was a hero of science." A policewoman said. "Don't you worry, he's been dead for decades."

"What's this guy's problem?" asked a male officer.

"Oh, he's harmless," the woman said. "It's just a bad case of paranoia. He's probably gotten out of one of the clinics, poor fellow doesn't even know where he is." She turned to face Edwin, a sad compassion in her eyes as she placed a hand on his shoulder, gently turning him away from the crowds. "Perhaps you should relax. Everything is going to be fine. Just sit and wait, while I call the hospital for you."

Breaking away from her grasp, Edwin ran, realising that a madman would not be tolerated for long in a place like Mare Serenitatis. Sure, the government here wasn't as totally controlling as on Earth, but a lunar colony only has so much air, so much available space. A lunatic would be more useful as a protein resource for the gardens than as a citizen. Somewhere, Edwin had read about the moon being a harsh mistress. He didn't want to find out how harsh.

In despair, Edwin decided he would return to his modest home. At least he would have his television to dull the pain of his failure. Edwin purchased a last-minute seat on a flight back to New Sydney, and boarded.

A few hours later, Edwin arrived home. The change had already begun. Muted monochrome walls, wherever such existed, were changing to vibrant colour displays. The cacophony was growing in intensity. All over Earth the advertisements were becoming brighter, louder, more insistent. What would the government be thinking? Were they fearing the increased exposure of their propaganda, or was the Department of Consumption gleefully rubbing its proverbial hands together in anticipation of an increased revenue?

Morbidly, Edwin feared what was to come, realising the hell he was accustomed to was likely to be replaced with one far worse. The blame settled on Edwin's shoulders like a leaded coat.

Rushing home, Edwin closed his front door as one of the outside walls flashed to that same irritating dancing child, this time in vivid colour. No doubt that upgrade would be inside soon. Subliminal messages had already guided his hand far more than he had ever imagined. What new horrors would he be responsible for?

With a dejected sigh, Edwin got himself a tall glass of whisky. He knew that wasn't the usual way of drinking the home-made alcohol, but he wanted to just forget the world, and a large drink of the potent stuff would help him achieve his goal. At least that was something he could control. Something he could believe was his own decision.

Taking a large sip, he sat in his armchair. Leaning over, he flicked the power on for the ancient black and white television. Entranced by his own malaise, Edwin Benedict was resigned to his fate in a sense of hopelessness.

On the television, in vivid clarity, a small child danced like a drunk elephant as the Cosper's Soda theme song played through the speakers.

About the Author:

M.R. Mortimer is an Australian Fantasy and Science Fiction writer. He is a former teacher, and an Anthropologist, living in rural NSW.

His available works include his Fantasy trilogy The Cinder Chronicles, several stand alone Science Fiction novels, and a short story collection. More information can be found on his website at suspendedearth.com.

Stepping Out

Christopher McMasters

\#

Stepping Out: The Personal Log of Captain Elizabeth
Sheridan, with an introduction by Jimena Ruiz, Secretary
General of the United Nations

<u>Introduction.</u>

After the exploratory ship *Fortitude* returned to Earth,
everything changed. The crew of the *Fortitude* had already taken
multiple Steps prior to the discovery of planet Kepler 76-e, now
known as Shackleton, or more popularly as 'The Shack.' It was
so named to reflect our own collective "Shackleton Moment,"
when the people of Earth wisely decided to turn back, to admit
that the prize, while worthy, was out of our reach, and the only
way to save humanity was to focus on our planet.

In 1908, Ernest Shackleton's prize was the South Pole. It
was a time of exploration, filled with toughened heroes, the
celebrities of their day. He could have continued and been

remembered as the first man to reach the pole. But he would have died on the return, just as his contemporary, Robert Scott, did a few years later.

Shackleton turned back, and in doing so, he saved his men. Similarly, we turned back, and in doing so, we saved ourselves. The crew of the *Fortitude* was in the depths of space for over sixteen years. Captain Elizabeth Sheridan had no way of knowing that the story of the Fortitude, of the disappointment the crew experienced, and the crushing despondency they felt when they decided to turn back, would have impacted humanity the way it did.

Kepler 76-e is the fifth planet orbiting a Sol-like star, located 2089 light-years from Earth. It is situated in the Goldilocks Zone, the habitable area around a star where the temperature is just right—not too hot and not too cold—for water to exist on a planet in liquid form. However, it wasn't merely water that the *Fortitude*, and many other exploratory ships, sought.

They were looking for life. Every planet so far discovered, and this is true to the present day, is devoid of life, even in fossilized form. Many of these planets contain water, both liquid and frozen, but none hold even the most primitive type of life. On our Earth, life first began over 3.5 billion years ago, maybe even over 4 billion years in the past. Not long after our oceans formed, microscopic single-celled organisms emerged, then grew and evolved into the myriad forms of life we celebrate today.

Early theories held that life on Earth might have come from biological matter carried by space dust or meteorites. We no longer believe this to be viable hypothesis. Earth is unique among trillions of planets orbiting billions of stars. Our Milky Way Galaxy, comprising over 200 billion stars, is itself one of perhaps two billion galaxies in the known universe.

And yet, as far as we can find, life is only known on planet Earth. Our home.

While Captain Sheridan and her crew Stepped back to Earth, despairing in what they perceived as their failure, today we see their discovery and voyage differently. Captain Sheridan, in her own words, "gave up." And when the *Fortitude* and its sole surviving crew member returned to Earth, we all, also, gave up. But in giving up, in losing hope that there was a new start or a sanctuary somewhere in the stars, we began to value what we had.

We will still reach out to the stars. We will still study and settle the planets we find, building new homes from bare rock, and mining their rich resources. We will still search for life. But not like before. Through her grief, Captain Sheridan helped us see that we need to value what we have. The planets that have been, and are still being discovered, can never provide enough to meet humanity's need for air to breath, land to farm, or oceans to fish. As news of the fate of the *Fortitude* spread around the globe, and especially after the publication of her personal log, Elizabeth Sheridan shocked a generation into action, initiating what would be known as *The Great Clean-Up*. During its time, it was called other things, with similar themes: the seventh generation, the waking up, a coming to our senses, taking responsibility, planning for a future. It was a true turning point—a pivotal decision.

I am honoured to write the introduction to this reprint of Captain Sheridan's brief log, a record she began to keep only after she and her crew realized that the beautiful green of The Shack one sees from space was only rock. Although she may not have known it at the time, what she penned was a wake-up call. I like to think that she knew, somewhere deep down, that that was what her words would become. She was the leader of the expedition, but also served as ship's doctor. Her deep concern for her crew fills her journal, but so too does her concern for those left behind on earth. It is nice to believe, if perhaps only a sentimental notion, that that was what motivated her to write them. If you are fortunate to view the original copy of her log kept at the United Nations Museum at Geneva, Switzerland, you will see that she did not date her entries. She seemed to let the pain inside her escape onto the page nearest to her pen at the time. This reproduction of her personal log has tried to stay true to how she wrote it.

Astrogator and astrophysicist Alan Seed was the only crew member of the *Fortitude* to return to Earth. As promised to Captain Sheridan, he shared the story of their exploration as well as her personal log. Their experience was not solitary. In the years immediately after the return of the *Fortitude*, other ships returned with core samples from barren rocky planets. None found the hoped-for sister to our home. Their failure mirrored that of the *Fortitude*, and personal accounts of their crew reflected the despondency felt by Sheridan and her crew. As more ships returned home, their logs were similarly published. But none had the effect of the first by the captain of the *Fortitude*. The return of the others gave it even more power.

We all owe her, and her crew, a great deal of gratitude. While Elizabeth Sheridan, and many of those with her, chose to 'step out' 2000 light-years from home, they will always be with us.

Jimena Ruiz,
Geneva, Switzerland

STEPPING OUT

The Personal Log of Captain Elizabeth Sheridan

I instructed the crew to cease geological surveys of the surface of Kepler 76-e. Nate refused. I have to find an opportunity to apologize to him. When I ordered the ground crew up, he said, "No. It's too soon."

I made myself listen to the recording. Then I deleted it from the record.

"It's not too soon," I told him. "It's already too late. It's time to go home."

For me, it is. I didn't quite know it on the bridge speaking to the survey crew at that moment, at least not consciously. But the decision brought relief.

Not to Nate. "No," he said. I could hear his anger; he didn't mask it. "What are you doing, *ordering* me?"

"Yes, Nate," I said. "Return to the ship so we can prep for return to the Ein-Ros[1]."

"No!" he said.

"This is an order, Mr. Huckins! Return to the ship."

"No. What are you going to do about it?"

We reduced ourselves to bickering children. The Captain and First Mate of an interstellar ship throwing tantrums. In hindsight, it's easy to remember that arguing with a child is a

---

[1] At the time of Captain Sheridan, Donuts were referred to as Ein-Ros, in reference to the Einstein-Rosen bridge the devices created. (Editor)

no-win situation. The child always wins. When there's no adult involved, it can only go badly.

"Refusing an order is mutiny!" I actually said that.

"Fuck you, Liz. This isn't the military."

I did the only thing I could. I shut up. Dead air filled the comms between us. Finally, I said, "Be careful down there[2]."

I waited for a reply, but none came. They would be back in two cycles; that's all they had supplies for. Forty-eight hours to clean up my mess. From his chair at navigation, Alan stared blankly at me, probably too confused or shocked to register what he just witnessed. At the time I wanted him to intervene, to take over, deem me unfit to continue command. I pleaded with my eyes, but he couldn't or wouldn't translate. Nobody wants to be in my shoes. I don't want to be in my shoes.

* * *

The survey party returned today. I went to Nate's cabin and stood in front of the door for several minutes, wanting to walk away, wanting to pretend what happened didn't. But I didn't have that kind of out. His door slid open when I knocked. He was standing in the middle of his cabin. I walked towards him, put my arms around him and he started to sob. Our tears soaked the backs of each other's necks. I don't remember

---

[2] The official log for this date consists of one line: *Survey party continuing work planetside.* There is no recorded evidence of this interaction. (Editor)

going to his bunk, but that is where we stayed, holding each other, crying.

* * *

The ship is quiet. Like a coffin. I gave instructions to Alan to plot the most efficient Steps home. It's likely all the crew feels the same way, but it is ultimately my decision. The responsibility is all mine. I am reassured by the lack of opposition. I expected more of a fight. At least an argument. Shouting. Storming out. But they just stared at me, resigned. They are tired of searching for something that none of us believe we will ever find. Nate almost looked sympathetic. They can all blame me.

Alan didn't look up from his work. He leaned over his screen, exploring trajectories, calculating fuel ratios, adjusting computations. Gary secluded himself in 'his' reactor room, prepping for acceleration. I tried to busy myself in the sickbay, tidying already orderly supplies. There's not much I could do. I've been too neat of a ship's doctor. I was tempted to reorder all medicines alphabetically—demerol, dextroamphetamine, diazepam, nitrazepam, temazepam, xylocaine. I put quite a few in their own cabinet and locked it. How will I hide the key from myself?

We move numbly. I fear when I can feel again, knowing where the key is. The cannabinoids are now in a glass-doored cabinet that used to house bandages, those with higher THC content to the front so they can be easily seen. Hopefully some will help themselves to this 'first aid.' I lack the ability to help myself. That is a sure sign of depression—having a helpful medicine at hand but not being able to bring myself to use it.

* * *

I sat on the bridge staring at the planet for hours. The green is the first I have seen, that any of us have seen since we . . . left. Why is that such a hard word to write? World after world of barren rock and poison air, of excitement and anticipation giving over to disappointment after disappointment.

Green. Fields of green, wrapping this lonely place. Dark and rich. Swaths of velvet. White clouds swirled in the atmosphere, winds dragging long tails over dark continents. A large spiralling storm formed a brooch on her green gown. If I didn't know how dead it was, I would have thought it so beautiful from here. Maybe it is, but I've seen far too many dead worlds to find beauty in any of them.

When I was a girl, there was a small field outside of town. I made the mistake of returning before leaving, visiting my old home, somehow knowing I would never return. It was gone. Built over. Dead. Dying, like the planet itself. It made me secure in my decision to leave Earth on the *Fortitude*. I would find a new home for all of us, a green place, a healthy place. Our first Step was so exciting. The anticipation, the exhilaration. Eight months building up to discovering nothing but a wind-blown rock. But we carried on. Another year sheltering from solar radiation behind an inner planet or moon while the Ein-Ros faced the star, absorbing and converting photons into the incredible amounts of energy needed. Then a Step, and another discovery. Deeper into the unknown. Another Step, farther than anybody had ever Stepped, and were rewarded with water![3] Dark rivers emerging from underground, flowing into vast alluvial plains and disappearing into fine sands, returning to its subterranean sea. Kristin spent weeks analysing it at the molecular level. But the results were the same. Devoid of any life. So, we kept going.

Green. Green. Green. Green. Green.[4]

I tried to remember what that field smelled like when I was a girl. I must have been sitting, eyes on the screen, for several hours. Alan startled me back to the moment, saying my name. He held out a mug of coffee and a handful of tissues. My cheeks were wet. Snot ran down my chin. I took the tissues and wiped my face. I tried to meet his eyes as I took the drink, but he was looking down. I think he was crying too.

* * *

Acceleration has increased gravity on the ship to 1.4. It mirrors our mood. The Ein-Ros is three months away. I am so heavy.

---

[3] The planet Captain Sheridan is referring to is HAT-P-5b, the colony planet known colloquially as 'Hat Pin'. Its rivers of clear water, underground caverns and resource rich minerals has enabled it to grow into a significant centre of mining and settlement. (Editor)
[4] This page in Captain Sheridan's original log is bordered in what looks like green pen. (Editor)

Weighed down. A leaden hand pushing from the centre of my heart, down, down, down. I fear all crew feels the same. It will be at least two weeks until we reach peak velocity and power down the reactor. So. Heavy.

* * *

The watch system has started to break down. I couldn't sleep, again, so I went to the bridge. Nate was alone. Kristin has not come out of her cabin for several cycles. Our dear astrobiologist. Her primary role was to study new life. She wanted to be the first to see it and study it. First contact, even if through a microscope. Every Step brought us all new levels of frustration and disappointment. To Kristin, astrobiology wasn't just about an evolutionary record, but the future of life in the universe. The future of our life in the universe. But all she found was . . . not death . . . but the lack of life. The impossibility of life. She tested algae and moss in the atmospheres, samples of the hardiest high-altitude plants from Earth. None survived. She developed an obsession with the rocks, grinding them ever smaller, insisting there was something 'between the molecules.' She'll have lots of time on the trip back to study it. If Dana gives her access to her core samples.

Gary is with the reactor all the time. There's none of his usual humour at the mess table. I don't even know if he's eating. I had to order him to let me in. He looks like he hasn't slept since . . . I don't know. He spoke in single words, and only in answer to questions. I gave him a sedative, a sleeping pill. He held it in his hand, looking confused. He caught me glancing at the reactor with a look of worry I didn't have the strength to hide.

"She'll be ok," he said. A hoarse whisper, an actual complete sentence. If he'd listen, I would confine him to sick bay. I'd confine all of us, force sedatives and sleep. But the chain of command seems to have broken down as well.

* * *

Kristin didn't answer my knocks at her cabin door. I overrode the lock, and when the door slid open, it was empty. Her bed was unmade. The room smelled of an unwashed body. Her papers had been strewn over the floor. Her notebooks toppled from a shelf as if they were thrown. Cynthia lay in the corner among broken glass and spilled soil. Each leaf of her *aspidistra elatior*[5] was sprinkled around her quarters, torn into smaller and smaller pieces. I searched the mess hall, the sickbay, the washroom, but could not find her. I called over ship's comms but got no response. I demanded the bridge answer. Dana eventually reported she was alone there. That she had not seen Kristin. Each answer had to be pulled out of her. I need to go to the reactor room. Gary will not reply.

---

[5] *Aspidistra elatior* is the Cast-Iron plant. Astrobiologist and Hydrologist, Kristin Vaughn brought her plant, which she named Cynthia, with her from Earth. She nursed it for the sixteen years she was on the *Fortitude*. (Editor)

* * *

The starboard outer airlock door was open. I wouldn't have noticed if I hadn't stopped to look into the only place I had not yet checked. The airlock is manually controlled from the inside and only operates if the inner door is sealed. From the inside. It could only have been done deliberately, by somebody determined to get out. The alarm would have to have been disengaged, which it was. I checked all the suits. One should be missing, but they are all there, hanging by each of our lockers.

Please, Kristin. Prove me wrong.

* * *

I assembled all crew in the mess. Kristin's seat was empty.

"Kristin has stepped out," I said. The conversation burned into my memory.

It was something we all knew, but the words had to be spoken aloud. To make it real. We sat as silently as tears ran down our cheeks.

"Like Oates[6]," Dana said. Softly. But we all heard.

"No, Dana," I said. "Not like that. Not like that all. We all feel bad. But stepping out is not saving anybody. Kristin wasn't

---

[6] Lawrence Edward Grace Oates accompanied Robert Falcon Scott on his ill-fated expedition to reach the South Pole. Afflicted with gangrene and frostbite, Captain Oates chose to die rather than be a burden to his companions, and thereby increase their chances of survival. He left his tent to freeze on the ice, saying as he went, "I am just going outside and may be some time." The story of the *Terra Nova* Expedition was among many of the books in the library of the *Fortitude*, and crew were quite familiar with their contents. (Editor)

holding us back. None of you are holding us back. We're not struggling to survive on some godforsaken icefield. We're just trying to get home. We're stronger together." I tried to sound like what I said held truth, but part of me envied Kristin.

The crew stared blankly at me. "Nobody is to be alone until I say. We need to rely on each other until we get through this. We can't be trusted by ourselves."

I was encouraged by the lack of resistance. "Nate and Gary will bunk and work together. Dana, you will partner with Alan."

"Clear?" I asked loudly, summoning an illusion of authority.

"Clear." Murmurs around the table.

"What about you?" Alan asked.

"I'll rely on all of you," I lied. "We'll remember Kristin when we flip for deceleration[7]."

After leaving the mess, I returned to the airlock. *Oh, Kristin.* I closed the outer door and secured the exit.

* * *

Flip and Decel. Preparations have kept us busy. Moving mass, inspecting the reactor. I assigned both teams to go over it, more to double-check Gary's work. The room is usually spotless, but there are worrying signs. Discarded food packets covered the

---

[7] There is no record in the official log of a ceremony being held for Kristin Vaughn, nor any other member of the crew. Just as Captain Sheridan's personal log became sporadic, with long periods of time elapsing between entries, the official ship's log similarly contained long periods with no entries. Only in the last three months of the return to Earth did astrogator and astrophysicist (and last remaining member of the crew of the *Fortitude*), Alan Seed, regularly record entries into the ship's log. (Editor)

floor. Glass panels were smudged with dirty fingers. Spilled mass. I had to leave the room before I lost control. Spilled mass! Infused deuterium pellets just lying about the deck! I felt so angry. Alan helped me go out, almost pushed me, and closed the door behind me.

Anger is a symptom of frustration. Frustration is a product of stress, of a lack of understanding. I remember the seminars before leaving. Psychologists speculating on what we might feel after years in space. They had no idea. *Use and develop the tools you can to show patience, acceptance, and trust.* Lucky for them now that they are so far away from me. So far away.

* * *

Hat-P5 grows larger in the viewscreen. We'll be docking with the Ein-Ros and leaving this system soon. Not soon enough. Once docking is complete Alan will go alone to initiate Step. He won't allow any other crew to join him in that inner sanctum. He never has.

* * *

I have to trust Alan in the control room, at the centre of the Ein-Ros, monitoring the quantum computer that is calculating our Step, his only company an AI that speaks in coordinates. Alan has been very withdrawn but speaks with me when I ask. Nate and Gary talk to each other quietly. It's not my imagination that they go silent whenever I am around, or when they notice I am near. I have nobody to talk to.

170

STEPPING OUT

* * *

Step. I usually dread the manoeuvre, the way it seems to stretch my body in all directions at the same time. Regardless, there used to be some anticipation, an excitement. Going farther than anyone has ever gone before. This time we're just trying to go back. Pointless pain. I don't even know what home is anymore. This ship has been my home. The crew, my family. Now the ship is only . . . a means to an end? An end none of us wanted? And my crew are like strangers. I don't even know myself anymore.

After the Step, Alan returned to the *Fortitude*. There was no celebration. No traditional drinks. No welcome back. No thanks. We only went backwards for the first time. We will wait behind an inner planet of another sun while the Ein-Ros recharges. Alan estimates it will take five months to collect enough power for the next step. He was plotted a four Step route back to Earth, utilizing maximum power to increase the distance of each Step. He has identified several larger G class stars with recorded exoplanets to shelter behind while the Ein-Ros builds up the power it needs. There is a risk the quantum computer can become damaged with the extra demands. But if it means a quicker way back, we all find the risk acceptable.

* * *

Freefall is making me weak. Floating like a ghost. It doesn't matter. I keep losing track of hours and cycles. We must be nearing time to re-join the Ein-Ros and Step. What will we tell them? That we failed? That nothing is out there? "Sorry guys, we couldn't save you. We're all going to die." I don't want to face that.

* * *

Nate and Gary are gone. They stepped out together. They hacked the starboard air lock. Gary left a note on the wall of the reactor room, but we can't make any sense of it. Gary probably couldn't either. Lines slanting down the page. The reactor room is a mess. Sqiggles of shit smear the walls. Globules of piss float in the air. Both he and Nate must have holed up in there, not even leaving to relieve themselves. I know I should feel more, I should cry or . . . anything. But I can't. And to be honest, I am glad I don't.

Dana is still talking to herself. She rolls her eyes and lapses into silence, but then snaps out of it and goes back to her conversation. Long babbling monologues that make no sense. Coaxing her to sick bay I tried to give her a sedative, but she swung her arm and hit me away. I floated to the bulkhead and hit my back on a cabinet. By the time I steadied myself, she was out the door.

* * *

Alan found Dana drifting in the loading bay, near her core samples.

We used the port airlock to dispose of her body.

172

STEPPING OUT

* * *

I had the dream again; at least I think it is a dream. I may not have been asleep. I am not always certain when I am. I was barefoot, walking on green grass. Each cold damp blade tickled the soles of my feet. They were young feet. Or I was young. Yes, I think I am young, a girl, back on Earth, back at home, in the field we used to visit. The sky is the palest blue. It is so beautiful. I breathe the warm, unfiltered air. I walk on. But the grass is becoming rougher. My feet are covered in dust, and the grass is coarse and dry. The sky has lightened, a burnt dirtied blue. I walk on until I come to a stream. There should be water. I know that it once was water. Only now it is a dark sludge. The smell is overpowering. But I walk closer, to the bank and step into the stream. My feet sink into gooey mud, but the mud burns. I step in deeper. The water reaches my knees, and then my thighs. My skin is in agony, burning, blistering, being eaten away. I go deeper still until I am chest deep, then neck deep. It is agony. I exhale slowly and then sink under the surface[8].

---

[8] Some have tried to find the field that Captain Sheridan describes from her childhood. They maintain that the dreams that plagued her were not from her own subconscious, but visionary glimpses of what would meet her upon return to Earth. The town where she grew up did have several parcels of open land around it before urban sprawl consumed them. The exact location of her childhood 'park' is unknown. A commemorative plaque has been placed near the location of the house where she grew up. The stream she describes was no different from most waterways in and around urban centres at the time. Whether a reflection of subconscious fear, or mystical glimpse into what awaited, it is commonly accepted that the recurring nightmares Captain Sheridan experienced during her last weeks on the *Fortitude* were a significant factor in her decision to step out. (Editor)

I write this down in the hope it will stop. I can still feel the burning.

* * *

The ship is on autopilot. It will dock with the Ein-Ros and then Step. Once in the solar system, it will detach, and accelerate towards Earth. Flip and Decel are programmed. Alan has promised to stay with the ship, to tell them what is out there, tell them to care[9]. He said he will do that for me. We sat together in the bridge, his hand resting on mine. We spoke with our eyes. I heard what he was feeling, and I am certain he heard me. That he understands why I am giving up. His smile was so soft, so gentle. He has been a rock. You know what I mean, Alan.

I am not as . . . brave as the rest of my crew. I am going to go to the medicine cabinet in sick bay and numb myself first.[10]

---

[9] Astrogator and astrophysicist Alan Seed honoured his promise to Captain Sheridan. He cooperated with the official investigation into the deaths of his crewmates, including handing over all confidential papers, such as the personal log of Elizabeth Sheridan. Three months after his return to Earth he stepped out, in his own fashion, and joined his Captain and crewmates. (Editor)

[10] This is the last entry in Captain Elizabeth Sheridan's personal log. (Editor)

About the Author:

Christopher McMaster lives beside the beach on the North Island of New Zealand. His debut, American Dreamer, *(part of a series of three published by Dreaming Big Publications) was released in late 2020. The second book in that series,* Tomorrow's History *(Jakob's Bidrag) was published in June 2021, with the third,* Gods and Dreamers, *to follow by year's end. He is currently working on his sixth novel, a climate fiction/science fiction story set in the fisheries of the near future.*

He has written and edited nine academic books, but finds much more pleasure in making stuff up.
Visit him at: https://christophermcmaster.com.